Dear Shrink

HELEN CRESSWELL

faber and faber

First published in 1982
by Faber and Faber Limited
3 Queen Square London WC1N 3AU
Photoset by Granada Graphics, Redhill, Surrey
Printed in Great Britain by
Redwood Burn Ltd., Trowbridge, Wiltshire

British Library Cataloguing in Publication Data

Cresswell, Helen
   Dear Shrink.
   I. Title
   823'.914 [J]   PZ7

ISBN 0-571-11912-3

To Win and Jim Wheable
with love

1

The worst part of any story is getting it started — that's when you're only *reading* a book, I mean. Sometimes when I open a book I've just picked out of the library or somewhere, I actually get quite a sick feeling at my stomach in case I don't make it. I really *hate* the first few pages of books. (Sometimes, I even hate the first chapters, but these are usually books somebody makes me read at school. If it were left to me, I'd just give up.)

This is the only book I've written, and I am truly terrified that you, whoever you are, will not get past *my* first pages. I feel excruciatingly helpless trying to get over to you that it will be worth it, it really will. I swear it. The ideal thing, I know, would be to start off with a murder: "Fascinated, he watched the slow spread of crimson staining the turf, as his old adversary's life blood ebbed away . . ." That sort of stuff. Or somebody hanging on to a cliff edge with cracking finger-nails. Or somebody getting on a plane to hi-jack it. Or how about this for an opener: "The two astronauts exchanged a long, hard look. This, they knew, was the moment of truth . . ." Some people might even say it would be a good idea to start with some teenagers taking drugs, but fashionable as this topic is supposed to be, I am not personally much riveted by this kind of scene. From my experience, nor are most of my friends. We know we are supposed to be, all right, but we just are not. (Except the odd one, like Terence Bratby, for instance, who is always making out that he knows millions of drug addicts, and has himself tried everything, including LSD. He talks this way because he is unsure of his own identity and wants to draw attention to himself, poor nut. We tend just to humour him.)

I have just read over what I have written so far and can see immediately that I have gone and done all the wrong things. I started, for instance, to get sidetracked on the subject of drugs. It's never good to sidetrack, and especially not in the first few pages.

So what I'll do, is give a brief summary of how the whole thing began, more or less as you would if you were writing a history essay, though what I have to tell is considerably more interesting than any history essay, I hasten to add, and has no resemblance to one.

My name is Oliver Saxon and I was thirteen at the time. Then there is my brother, William, who was nearly sixteen, and my kid sister, Lucy, who was seven. (There is a big gap between Lucy and me because my parents had been meaning to only have two children, and then changed their minds. This is not all that unusual. We know one family with *five* children where the parents only meant to have two, and then kept changing their minds.)

My mother and father are both botanists, and that is how all the trouble really started. Botanists are people who are interested in studying plant life. I mention this because sometimes I've been asked what this word means, which shows that it is not all that well known.

I realize that talking about things starting with plants and flowers is not in the same category as starting with a murder or a hi-jacking, and if some of you give up reading now I will not really blame you. I can see that it does not seem to hold much hope of excitement. But I will mention that although things sound pretty calm at the moment, we Saxons are shortly thrown into the swirling torrent of life and undergo grief, terror and misery of every kind. I really mean this. If any of you have ever read *Oliver Twist*, or *Roots*, it might give you some idea of what is to come.

For you to understand just how unprepared we were for the doom that was to befall us, I must first describe how we were before my parents went missing in the Amazon jungle. (This is a fact. They really did.)

We led what people call a "sheltered" life. I realize this now, but did not at the time. I don't believe people ever think about the kind of lives they lead until something happens to shake them up, as it did ours. We just took everything for granted. We were happy, I suppose, but there again, you don't think of yourself as happy until you're not any more. We certainly seemed to laugh a lot in those days.

One thing I will mention and then pass over quickly is that we also had quite a lot of money compared with most people. I suppose this must be because botanists make a lot of money, especially if they write books, and we had two of them in the family. So it was not really our fault. If there is one thing I really hate it is people who

11

think that just because they've got a Jaguar car (which we had not, I hasten to add) or a crummy swimming pool in the garden or something, this is some kind of a big deal, and makes them about a million times better than anybody else (except other people with Jaguars and swimming pools, of course). I'm not saying that *everybody* with Jaguars and swimming pools is like this, because they are not. I am just saying that from what I have seen, a lot of them are, and I want to let you know that our family was definitely not in this category. My parents had faults, all right, but this was not one of them.

Anyway, I'll just tell you about William and Lucy, and then get right into the action, I swear I will. There is not really much to tell, and you will get to know them both for yourselves in the end. I will just mention that William tends to be rather cool, calm and collected, and is probably better than I am in times of crisis, when I tend to become somewhat excitable. (My mother used to say over-excitable, but this of course was just her opinion.)

Lucy is a really great kid, and makes me laugh more than anyone I know. She's very skinny, but in a nice way, not the way where people's bones all stick out. Dainty skinny, I suppose you might say, if this does not sound too wet. She's really pretty as well, though she doesn't realize this, thank heavens. The minute girls realize they're pretty they've had it, in my experience. This is why I quite often call her "Ugly-mug" and I sometimes call her "Albertine" as well, though don't ask me why. She uses a lot of long words and can do impressions of all the pop stars bang-on — I wish you could see her doing the Boom Town Rats and Kate Bush. It would kill you. Even my friends, when they came round, used to get her to do Kate Bush. Another person she can do is Margaret Thatcher. Everyone thinks I've trained her up to do this, but I swear I didn't. She just picked it up herself. Her hair helps, because it's very fair and curly, and she kind of rocks to and fro with her hands clasped and she says this little speech about "Ladies and gentlemen. I am here today to talk to you about politics. As you know, I find politics absolutely fascinating." Then comes the bit that really kills me, when she gets Tories mixed up with tourists. "I am, as you know, a tourist, and next week I shall be going on my holidays with President Ronnie Reagan to Majorca. I hope to find the experience absolutely fascinating."

It doesn't look much, when you just write it down in cold blood, but to see that skinny little kid just standing there doing it in deadly earnest, is really something. Everyone I've ever known has said so.

So that's the family. And how it started was by my parents fulfilling their lifelong ambition to go to the Amazon jungle and study the plant life there and write a book about it. This was something they had always wanted to do and obviously they couldn't take us kids.

Now before you start thinking what kind of selfish people they were to take off for the Amazon and abandon their helpless children, I must emphatically say this was not so. They had devoted most of the best years of their lives to bringing us up, and the only time they had ever left us before was once when they went to Austria for a month. And it is no use pretending that that did any of us any harm, because Lucy can't even remember it, and all I remember is that we had a great time staying with our grandmother, who was still alive then. (Well — obviously!) We now, I regret to say, have no grand-parents, and no other real relations either, both my parents being only children.

I realize that in the first few pages of a book is not the place to go into the rights and wrongs of only children, though in this case it does have a bearing on things. We could have done with some aunts and uncles, as things turned out. We had one another, all right, when our troubles started, but we are all minors. In our opinions we could have looked after ourselves perfectly OK, but under law minors have to be in proper care and protection whether they like it or not. There is absolutely nothing you can do about this, as we discovered to our cost.

As soon as our parents began to talk about the trip, the first thing we said was that we could look after ourselves.

"I could be legal guardian," was what William said, but not a single one of us agreed with that. Lucy and I knew full well that all this meant was that he'd be able to boss us around even more than usual. My mother said, "Don't be silly, dear. You're not even sixteen till next year."

Dad had the idea that we could all go and stay with friends, but there were two big snags to this. The first was that there wasn't anyone we knew who was willing to take all three of us for at least six months. There were people who would take all of us for around a fortnight, and one or two people who at a pinch would have taken just one of us for the whole six months. But no one would go the whole hog. I honestly don't think you could blame people for this.

Anyway, the other snag was the main one. All three of us were against the idea of being farmed out. We wanted to stay in our own house. At first, it was only Lucy who said this, but in the end we all admitted it. After all, six months is a long time, and it could even turn out to be longer. When your parents aren't there, at least it's something to have your own room and your own things. Lucy spends hours on her own in her bedroom, playing complicated games with Lego and Scalectric and furry toys. You can hear her in there, doing all different voices, in fact sometimes it's a temptation to creep up and listen at the door. I never do, though. It wouldn't seem fair. The point is, with her being the youngest she was the one who would miss Mum and Dad most, and she was going to need all those toys and private games. She couldn't do it in someone else's house.

I don't mind admitting that I spend a lot of time in my own room as well, one way or another. I read, and play records, and listen to the radio, and practise my guitar, and so on.

"I quite take your point," Dad said when I mentioned this. "I can't see anybody taking you *and* your guitar for six months. Nor for six days, if it comes to that."

This wouldn't have been a bad crack if it had been the first time he'd ever said it, but he'd said it about six hundred times before, so I treated it with the contempt it deserved.

"We shall have to get someone to live in," Mum said.

"Like who?" Dad asked.

"Somebody sensible and reliable. Someone who can clean and cook and make things go as they should."

"Like who?" Dad asked again.

"If one of them were to be ill, I should want to know that someone responsible was right on hand."

Mum doesn't pay all that much attention to Dad, though she's not as bad as the mother of a boy I used to know. He told me that one morning his mother was rabbiting on about the price of vegetables, and his father kept saying, "I feel terribly funny", and "I think I might be going to faint", and that sort of thing. Anyway, to cut a long story short, she just went waffling on about tomatoes being fifty pence a pound or whatever they were, and when she turned round, there he was on the floor, dead. It was a heart attack, this boy said. I think it's pretty terrible when people won't listen even when you're trying to tell them you think you're going to die. I think it's really frightening.

"Like who?" Dad said again.

"Well . . ." She seemed to have heard, this time. "Who do you think?"

"Think?" he said. "I can't think of a single person we know who would move in here and take this lot on. For love or money."

"Oh, don't be silly, John," she said. "Of course there must be."

"Like who?" he said.

It was getting excruciatingly boring.

"I can't think of *anybody* I want to move into my house," Lucy said.

I liked that — *her* house.

16

"I just wish you weren't going. We might get someone like a wicked stepmother. We might get someone who would poison us."

Old Lucy's like that. She's got this strong sense of the dramatic. That's what it said once on her school report. You can tell she's got a strong sense of the dramatic by those noises I was telling you about that you hear coming from her room, and her doing about a dozen different voices, as if she was putting on a one-man *Hamlet* or something. And she reads a lot of books and gets influenced by them. She must obviously have been reading some book about a wicked stepmother who tried to poison some children, though I'm bound to say I can't think where she'd get hold of a book like that. It's not exactly what I'd read to a seven-year-old kid like Lucy. The trouble is, she's got this fantastic reading age, and can read just about anything. My parents tried to remember to hide the newspaper since the day she read about a prostitute being found naked and dismembered on some waste ground, and read it out at breakfast and wanted it explained. But you can't protect her from everything. The funny thing is, she never gets scared by any rubbish she sees on television, only by what she reads. She can see straight through television, old Lucy can.

I talked her out of the poisoning scare by offering to be her taster, if anyone came along who looked the poisoning type. I explained all about Lucrezia Borgia and the Roman emperors and the Beefeaters, and she got really interested in the whole subject. By the time I'd finished, you could see that she'd almost be disappointed if a poisoner didn't turn up.

My mother advertised in the local papers for someone to come and live in at our house while they were away. I saw the ad. It said: "Kindly, respectable housekeeper/cook required for a min. six months from September, to live in and look after three well behaved children 7-15, generous wages and all found."

We only got two replies. One was from a lady who was a vegetarian and had two pekingese dogs. Mum said she wouldn't do, because we three needed our protein, and the dogs would make the house smell. I didn't see the second, but Mum said that she drank.

"There you are then," William said. "So I'll be legal guardian. The most I ever have is a couple of lemonade shandies."

Mum was not really in a laughing mood, though. She was torn. On the one hand she had this lifelong ambition to botanize in the Amazon — "Your father and I are not getting any younger, you know," she told us, and I suppose that was true. Unarguable. But on the other hand, she could not abandon us children to just any old vegetarian who drank.

Things were getting considerably desperate when she had this sudden idea about someone who'd looked after her, when she was a child. It was somewhere in the country, in Oxfordshire, and Mum started making 'phone calls and doing all kinds of detective work, to track this old lady down. (She must have been pretty old if she looked after Mum.)

Anyway, in the end she did track this Mrs Bartle down, and the way she carried on you'd have thought

18

she'd tracked down Captain Scott alive and well at the North Pole. She said this Mrs Bartle was a widow now, and her children were grown up and married, and that she would come the very next day on the train and see if we would suit.

Naturally we were pleased for Mum's sake, but the way she made us all scurry round was a bit much — tidying our rooms and washing our hair and moving William's skeleton out of the hall, and so forth.

"Elderly ladies do not relish reminders of mortality," she told William. (This is the way she talks, my mother.)

Still, she seemed happy, bustling about and going on and on about her golden childhood with this Mrs Bartle, about picking redcurrants and gooseberries and gathering buttercups and tasting the scones before they went in the oven, and being allowed to stir in the currants and sultanas. We all thought this considerably overdone. It sounded like an ad. for marge, or something. Still, it was no skin off our noses, as there wasn't much chance of *our* being made to pick buttercups and such.

She kept calling this Mrs Bartle "a kindly soul", and I think was getting confused in the mists of time. I can honestly say I've never in my life met anyone I could describe as "a kindly soul", at least, not outside books. She made her sound like a cross between Nana in *Peter Pan* and Peggotty in *David Copperfield*. At any rate, she sure as hell didn't sound like any poisoner.

2

Dad went to the station to meet Mrs Bartle and while he was gone the rest of us sat round and felt as jumpy as if we were waiting for the dentist. Mum was more nervous than anybody. She was like a frog on a hot stone. This was partly because she knew her whole Amazon trip was at stake, but also partly, I think, because she was hoping that we would live up to Mrs Bartle's expectations.

It never really seemed to cross her mind that Mrs Bartle would not live up to *our* expectations, and I am bound to say that in my case, she certainly did not. A lot can happen in thirty years, and in my opinion a lot had happened to her.

When we heard the car in the drive Mum rushed out and we all sat and made faces. Then she came back in leading this old lady dressed all in black.

I am now at an awkward juncture. I know that in real life you should not make personal remarks about people — especially their appearance, which all too often they cannot help. But in a book it is the author's duty to describe to the reader people who play a big part in the story, and you have to do this very honestly. I mean, it would be no use, for instance, mincing your words about Frankenstein's monster, or there would be no point in the story.

I am not of course saying that Mrs Bartle looked like Frankenstein's monster, but she was certainly a sorry disappointment. To start with her appearance. She was what you might call stout, but what I think was actually fat. She was fat enough to make her breathless, and to make her eyes, which for all I know were perfectly normal-sized, look very small. Her hair was nearly white, and so were the little whiskers on her chin. And as to her clothes, you could see that she had not moved with the times.

But the really depressing thing was that you could tell Mum was disappointed in her as well. To disguise this, she was being considerably gay and bright and asking inane questions about Mrs Bartle's married daughters, but you could see the gulf yawning between them. Mrs Bartle hardly seemed to be listening, and was all the time looking round the room, taking it all in. All of us were being desperately polite for Mum's sake.

While we were having tea, Mrs Bartle opened up a bit and talked about how lonely she was these days. Mum picked that up like a shot.

"Well, you certainly wouldn't be lonely here!" she said.

"Have you got the television?" Mrs Bartle asked. "Colour?"

"Oh yes!" Mum practically shrieked. "And of course it is perfectly understood that whatever programmes you wish to watch, the children will fall in with."

I realized at once that this probably meant we would have to spend hours huddled round the little portable upstairs to watch anything decent. Lucy opened her mouth and I was terrified she was going to say something like,

"What about Top of the Pops and the Incredible Hulk?"

But she closed her mouth without saying anything, to my relief. It sounds silly now, but at the time I was so nervous that I actually got up and switched on the television set to show her the picture. It was a crazy thing to do, and the rest just stared at me.

The funny thing was, Mrs Bartle didn't. She leaned forward and looked really interested for the first time.

"What a lovely picture!"

I then turned it off quickly in case she got interested in what was on, and it killed the conversation. Not that the conversation was exactly scintillating.

"You obviously enjoy the television then, Barty," my mother said.

Now Mum had told us before how she used to call her Barty in the good old gooseberry-picking and currant-scone days, but she certainly hadn't come out with it that afternoon, and when she did, just like that, my blood more or less froze. I hardly dared look at Mrs Bartle to see how she'd taken it. I didn't need to. I don't think she even noticed. She just started on about a whole list of her favourite programmes and in fact brightened up for the first time. She was reeling off a list of terrible stuff she always watched. Some of it I'd never even heard of, and apparently it was in the afternoons.

It was then that the sad side of her life struck me. There is something sad when people's husbands die and their

22

daughters go and get married and they are left watching television, even in the afternoons. And I saw that this was why there was something so faraway about her, because we were in real life, and she wasn't. If she came and looked after us for six months, then perhaps this would bring her back into real life again, and this would change her back into how she was when Mum knew her, and she would be really happy and grateful. The idea of this appealed to me at the time.

"I hope you *will* come, Mrs Bartle," I said. "Mum says you used to be a really great cook. And I bet you still are, with all those cookery programmes, and everything."

"Well, dear, I must say I always did enjoy a good bake. Not that I always send off for the recipes and leaflets, because there isn't much call for me to bake these days."

"Ah, but there would be," I said cunningly. "We all eat masses of cakes and puddings." (White lie — we would if we could, but Mum doesn't altogether approve.)

"Can you make lemon meringue pie, Mrs Bartle?" Lucy asked.

"When I used to make lemon meringue pie," she said, "it'd be all wolfed up before I'd hardly finished scraping the dish."

"Oooh!" said Lucy. "That sounds lovely."

It was as if everything was settled from then on. Mrs Bartle had decided that she would enjoy watching our television and then cooking the recipes for us, and we had decided that we would enjoy eating them. This may seem a superficial way of deciding something important, but after all, what else was there to go on? Mrs Bartle didn't know us and we didn't know her, and it was not as if she was adopting us for life. It was only going to last six months and we would manage. That was how it seemed at the time.

It was amazing how everybody suddenly cheered up. Mum took her upstairs and showed her the room she was to have, and she really liked it. Lucy went up with them, and told me afterwards.

"The main thing she liked was the big windows. She said her house only had little windows, and that her eyes weren't very good these days."

"I'm not surprised, all the telly she watches," I said.

"And she liked the way she'd got her own bathroom leading straight off. She thought the bathroom was really lovely. I think I'm going to like her."

I nearly said, "Yes, but is she going to like *us*?" but stopped myself in time. It was one thing for her to like the telly and her bathroom, but she hadn't up to now, to be truthful, shown all that much interest in us. This could well be because she had gone rusty about caring about people. And as far as I was concerned, I didn't mind this, and nor would William, who hadn't even wanted anybody to come. Even if she ignored us for the whole six months, it would be no skin off our noses.

But Lucy was different. Apart from being only seven, she is a very affectionate little kid and needs a lot of affection back. She even hugs me a lot and gets me to read to her in bed, and so on, and I certainly hoped Mrs Bartle was going to get fond of Lucy, to make up for Mum and Dad not being there. I reckoned she would, because I didn't see how anybody could not get fond of Lucy. Mrs

24

Bartle would not necessarily go for her imitations, and the way she goes off into the giggles, but apart from anything else she has a kind heart. When she thinks Mum is sad or something, she goes and picks flowers and arranges them for her, and once she spent her whole week's pocket money on a pot donkey for Dad to look at while he lay in bed with 'flu. That sort of thing. She also gets very upset about people in famined lands and so on, when Blue Peter has appeals, and rakes the whole house looking for buttons or stamps or keys or whatever it is. She once sent off a ring of Mum's that was worth quite a lot of money and there was a considerable row about this. Lucy really flew at Mum, and told her how mean it was to grudge one mouldy ring to starving people, when she has about a hundred more. She kept stamping her foot and screaming and in the end rushed up to her room and banged the door. When she came out she was crying, and offered to write to Blue Peter and ask for the ring back, but Mum wouldn't let her. She said Lucy was quite right, but she should have asked her permission first. And then she took her to the film of *Watership Down* to cheer her up. (Not that it did. She cried buckets all the way through that as well.)

After Mrs Bartle's visit, and everything now being arranged, things really seemed to snowball. Mum and Dad spent their whole time getting their equipment together and making long 'phone calls and having hundreds of jabs. After one of these Dad's arm came up like a balloon and the doctor even came. I was glad when he got over this, because John Parsons told me that he had once nearly died of a smallpox vaccination. He, mind you, is exactly the type who would. If you gave him a glass of water and told him it was vitriol, he would probably die after the first mouthful. Autosuggestible.

The last week in August we went to a hotel in Lyme Regis for a holiday. We don't often go to hotels because we have this place in Shropshire where we usually go, mainly because of the plant life. We call it the Shack because it's only made of wood, and is right at the end of a cart track. Half the time we can't even get the car up to it because of the mud. We always like going there, but going to a hotel somewhere different was a real treat, which is what it was meant to be, of course. The food was really good, and while we were there Mum and Dad were interviewed on television about their trip, and their photos were in the papers, so we were quite celebrities. I had always rather looked down on celebrities, thinking they were phonies, but no one could accuse my parents of being phonies, so there seemed no reason not to enjoy it. Also, it made their going away seem like a real adventure for the first time, and not quite so sad.

There are millions of fossils at Lyme Regis, and we all got interested in them, especially Lucy, who kept going off on her own and stamping on rocks and commanding dinosaurs to come forth. Even by the end of the week she hadn't given up doing this. Somewhat of an optimist. She lugged tons of fossils back with her to the hotel, and put them in rows under her bed until the hotel people complained. We ended up with them all in the boot of the car, with the result that Dad said it took us an hour longer getting home than it had coming.

26

The last three days at home were very queer. The whole thing was suddenly on us, and it was as if we had never really prepared for it at all. There were trunks and crates lined up in the hall, and hundreds more 'phone calls and none of our meals were at the proper times. It was like spending three days in a station waiting for a train. On the day before my parents left, Mrs Bartle arrived. This was obviously a good idea, so that Mum could show her the ropes, and so forth, but in another way it was bad, because that last day we never really had Mum and Dad to ourselves at all. Even on that last evening we did not have a proper leavetaking. It is impossible to have a family farewell when there is an almost total stranger there. Afterwards, I used to think a lot about this, and regret it bitterly. Proper goodbyes are always important.

3

The first few days were the worst. We still had four days before we went back to school, so we were all thrown in at the deep end. It must have been just as awkward for Barty as it was for us. We were already calling her Barty among ourselves, and then one night when Lucy was being put to bed, I heard her asking if we could call her that.

"It sounds more friendly," she said.

"You could always call me Auntie Emily. That's my name — Emily."

Funnily enough, I'd never thought of her as having a Christian name. Some people are like that. You can think of them as Mr or Mrs or Miss Somebody or other, but not as someone with an actual name. What this shows I don't know.

"Thank you very much, but I'd rather not," I heard old Lucy say. She said it very politely. "I always think it's peculiar to call people Uncle and Auntie when they're not. There's a girl in my class who calls nearly all her mother's friends Auntie, and I've told her millions of times how ridiculous it sounds. I mean, if I were going to call you by your *Christian* name, I'd just call you Emily, plain Emily. But I think you're too old for me to call you by your Christian name. The age gap is too big. But can we call you Barty, like Mummy did?"

Old Barty muttered something back, and I heard Lucy say, "Oh good!" You could tell Lucy was running rings round her in there. I don't suppose either of her two daughters had been anything like Lucy. She even got Barty to read her some of *The Wind in the Willows*. She's always getting people to read her that. She's perfectly capable of reading it herself, and in fact has done so about a hundred times. She practically knows it off by heart. Unfortunately, Barty didn't seem to be a very good reader. She kept putting the emphasis on the wrong words. And she didn't enter into the spirit of the thing, and do the proper voices for Ratty and Toad. So it ended up with Lucy reading it to her. Then, just as she was getting warmed up, Barty said,

"I'd better be off downstairs now, or I shall miss my *Crossroads*."

I thought this considerably bad-mannered, not to mention stupid. Anyone who prefers that crummy programme to Lucy reading *The Wind in the Willows* has got to be stupid. Anyway, I went in there after Barty had gone down and we read a whole chapter.

Then I went down and sat with Barty, because it seemed rude to leave her on her own during that first week. William, naturally, was out. I have forgotten to mention the fact that William was in love. He had told me this about three weeks previously, and I was pretty astonished, because William had never really shown much interest in girls. And when he told me, he was dead serious about it. And he didn't say, "There's this bird I fancy," or anything like that. "I'm in love." That's what he said. Real Romeo and Juliet stuff. Her name was Carol Evans and I hadn't seen her yet, but apparently she had the most incredible black silky hair and big brown eyes. He was obviously absolutely soppy about her and was copying out love poems and sending them to her. He hadn't made up any of his own, as far as I knew (though he wouldn't have shown them to me, even if he had). He's not the type. I can write poetry if I feel like it, thought I'm bound to say I've never written a poem about a girl. But William is basically very down to earth, and the mere fact that he was even copying out poems was amazing. I didn't even know he knew what poetry was. He said that he was going to marry her, though I did point out that this was rather premature.

So there I was stuck with old Barty and the telly, and it was considerably depressing. For one thing you could hear her breathing — sort of wheezing — and for another, she was eating sweets and biscuits the whole time. And she didn't eat them in a very quiet way. Of course, as she had been living on her own for so many years, I suppose she didn't have to bother about not annoying people by making sucking noises and eating with her mouth open. I may be unusual, but this sort of thing drives me nuts. If somebody even starts scrunching an apple I usually leave the room until they've finished, and I wouldn't dream of crunching one myself unless everybody else was as well. In the end, I got a toffee and started making sucking noises myself, partly to drown out her noises, and partly to see if she'd take the hint. She didn't even notice. She just carried on

30

crunching and sucking as if she were being paid to. About nine o'clock she suddenly seemed to remember I was there, and said, "What time do you have supper?"

I told her that we didn't have supper, as such, and the way she gaped at me, you'd have thought I'd said that we never had baths. She said that she always had some bread and cheese, or a tin of soup or something, so I offered to go and get it for her.

"Oooh! It's me that's supposed to be looking after you!" she said, though you could see that she was pleased.

"Not exactly looking *after*," I told her. "I mean, just keeping an eye on us. We aren't the type to be waited on hand and foot. When we're at the Shack, we haven't even got electricity."

"Well I never! What's the Shack, then, dear? Is it a little den you have to play in?"

I'm afraid that this was another of the troubles with Barty. I'm sorry to seem so criticial, especially in the light of later events, but she never really seemed to grasp how old we were. She didn't even treat Lucy as her age. And when William or I would be going out in the evening, she'd say, "Children aren't children five minutes these days!" If she said that once, she said it a million times.

I got her some bread and cheese and made a pot of tea, and I had some as well out of politeness. I told her a bit about the Shack, but not too much, because she couldn't seem to understand why anyone would think it fun to go and stay there. So I told her about the hotel in Lyme Regis instead, and she enjoyed that better, even if she did have one eye the whole time on some awful

31

American movie about two hundred years old.

By the time I went to bed I had done my duty up to the eyeballs, I thought. I decided that it would not be incumbent on me to keep her company in this way every night, just on her first night. For one thing, good manners didn't demand it, and for another I didn't think she would necessarily appreciate it. You only spend a lot of time in someone else's company if you have a lot in common. William came in not long afterwards and seemed in a depressed mood. He said it was just his luck that Barty should move in now, because he'd been on the point of bringing Carol home to meet Mum and Dad. Apparently she'd seen the television interviews and things in the newspapers and so on, and said she was really interested in meeting them.

"We've got to go somewhere in the evenings, anyway," he said. "It's getting dark by half past six, and we can't go to her house all the time, and we sure as hell can't afford to keep going to the movies or somewhere."

"I don't see why you can't bring her here," I said. "You can warn her about Barty beforehand. She won't hold her against you."

"It makes me feel an idiot, having to be babysat by her. I *told* them we didn't need anyone, and we didn't."

"She's not that bad. Though, Gordon Bennett, you should hear her sucking and clacking her teeth around! She ate sweets and biscuits non-stop. When you bring Carol round, you want to just introduce her, and then bring her up here. You'll have to, anyway, if you want to play the stereo or watch anything decent on telly."

The next week he did bring Carol round. Lucy was

skipping about by her window waiting to catch a sight of her. She thought it was all truly romantic.

"William is bringing his true love home!" she kept chanting. In the end I told her to shut up. She'd got herself togged up in a decent dress, for once. She goes through phases of being all girly and Goldilocks, and then the next minute looks an all-out scruff for weeks on end. She was in her T shirt, plimsolls and dungarees phase at the moment, so putting on a dress was definitely a gesture in this Carol's honour.

"Oooh, look — they're here! Hasn't she got long hair? Hair as black as a raven's wing!"

We were all introduced to Carol together. I naturally did not stare, but am afraid the same can't be said of the other two.

Barty said, "Delighted, I'm sure."

Conversation was awkward, to put it mildly. Barty asked Carol how old she was, and then which school she went to and then, would you believe, what time she had to be home! You could see that William was just about ready to sink through the floor. How they got out of the room in the end I don't remember, but they did, and Lucy and I followed after a decent interval.

When we got upstairs Lucy started to tiptoe along the landing towards William's room, but I dragged her back into mine and shut the door.

"What d'you think you're playing at, nosy little kid!"

"Leave me alone!" she hissed at me. She's got a real temper, Lucy has. "If you must know, I was going to listen to see if I could hear low murmurs and sounds of kissing."

33

I burst out laughing. I mean, I had to, hearing it put like that. And then she started giggling, and both of us rolled on the bed and stuffed the cover in our mouths and were more or less helpless for a bit. Even when we did talk, it had to be muffled, for fear of William hearing and getting embarrassed.

"*Will* they be kissing?" Lucy whispered in the end. Her face was bright red and wet with giggling.

"I dunno. Probably."

This set her right off again, and I must admit it did me too. This sounds a bit childish on my part, and I tried to think afterwards about why it had had this effect on me. Partly it was just infectious, of course. You get one person giggling, especially Lucy, who is champion of the world at this, and everybody else sets off. But partly it really *was* the thought of William being just along the landing in his room, kissing this girl. I admit it. If you'd known old William all your life, and were his brother, like I am, and had had mumps and measles at the same time, I think it would have had this effect on you as well. I can remember that room when the whole floor was covered in scalectric. And even now the walls are covered with posters of America — New York, mainly, which is where he says he's going to live when he's qualified as an architect.

Personally, I think this is nuts, and have told him so. If anywhere on earth doesn't need architects, it's New York. Even I could design a skyscraper — even Lucy could, for heaven's sake. You can't tell one skyscraper from another, everyone knows that. No one is ever going to make a name designing *those*. I mention that as well, because William intends to be a *famous* architect, he says. Anyway, he knows my opinion. The only way to get a skyscraper noticed in New York, is to put King Kong on the top of it.

The point is, that I really absolutely could not *imagine* William in there among his posters and hi-fi actually kissing that girl. It really made my mind boggle. And mixed in with that (since I've been analysing my reactions) I suppose I felt a bit sad about it. If once William had started kissing girls, it put a barrier between us. It was a Great Unmentionable. I knew he would never talk to me about it, and he never did. And also I could sense that that girl, whom I'd never even seen before tonight, was more important to him than I was, or Lucy, or even Mum and Dad, for all I knew. And this made me feel outraged, in a way, as if all the family years had been thrown out of the window at a stroke, as if they didn't count for anything at all. I'm probably putting this badly. William and I have always got on all right, but I don't want to give the impression we were twin souls, or anything. No way.

But I could certainly now see how parents must feel when their kids suddenly go and fall in love with complete strangers. I know kids don't *belong* to their parents, but it must be pretty hard for parents to feel that they don't, in a way. After all, you've got to admit that they create the kids in the first place. And then they spend years spoon-feeding them and changing nappies and tending every want. If they didn't, all children would perish, even in this day and age. In ancient civilisations any baby that was born malformed, or if it was a girl and the parents had wanted a boy, was what they called "exposed". What this meant was that it was taken and left on a hillside, where it perished. There is no way a baby would not perish if abandoned by its parents, on a hillside or anywhere else. The only case you ever hear of where they do not, are in ancient myths, like Romulus and Remus, who were suckled by a she-wolf, or Mowgli. And even this has to be taken with a pinch of salt. A sack of salt, in my view.

So parents must really love their children to do all this hard work in bringing them up, and it does seem a bit unfair that in the end, when the children have grown up, they don't love their parents back. At least, they may, but not necessarily. Take Barty's daughters. If their childhood was anything like as golden as Mum makes out hers was when she was with her, all buttercups and sunshine and sultana scones, you'd have thought they'd still have felt pretty affectionate toward her now. I'm not saying *I* thought she was all that lovable — I didn't have to, she wasn't my mother. But these two (one's called Barb, by the way, and the other Janet) didn't seem to care tuppence for her. From what I could make out they never even wrote, and they only rang once in a blue moon. And this Barb apparently sent Barty a green scarf on her birthday (two weeks late), forgetting that she was superstitious about green. She'd never worn green in her entire life, Barty said. This is because her father wore a green shirt one day and was crushed under a tractor This doesn't seem a very good reason to me, but it did to her. Other people's superstitions always seem silly, but I think you've got to respect them.

Anyway, the point I'm making is that if this Barb didn't know after all these years that her mother never wore green, and wouldn't even if you paid her a thousand pounds, she said, it did show lack of affection. Perhaps Barb was too busy giving her own kids a golden childhood among the buttercups, though I doubted it. And even if she was, the whole thing did seem a kind of vicious circle.

The above thoughts I was not thinking at the actual time Lucy and I were giggling, but later, probably when I was in bed. I tend to use quite a lot of time thinking when I'm in bed, because there is not always a lot of opportunity for this during the day. On this occasion, I certainly couldn't have done much thinking at the time, because the most awful thing happened. Lucy and I had left off discussing William and were playing Monopoly. I don't know how much later this was exactly, but we were just at the stage when most of the property had been bought and I think I'd just put my first house on the Bond Street lot. Then all of a sudden we heard old Barty shouting. Perhaps not shouting — not yet — but calling up the stairs. We couldn't hear exactly what she was saying, but it was obvious that she wanted us, so Lucy jumped up like a grasshopper and opened the door.

"Hello, Barty! We're up here! We're playing Monopoly."

"Where's William?" I could hear Barty. "He's not in the other room." She always called the study "the other room". "Has he gone out without telling me?"

"Oh no! It's all right. They're in his room. They're playing records, I think. And Oliver and me are playing

Monopoly, and I've got *all four* stations!''

What followed then was almost too awful to describe. I don't think I'd ever been more embarrassed in my life. Barty started thumping up the stairs, you could hear her gasping for breath and words puffing out in between, like ''disgusting'' and ''disgraceful''.

By the time she got to the top of the stairs, William had heard her as well. There we all were, Lucy and me in my doorway and William in his, and Barty puffing and gasping. Her face was red and her eyes were mad but also shifty, and not looking straight at anyone, as if she was as embarrassed as any of us. It's difficult to remember exactly what she shouted.

''All the time me sitting there, thinking you were next door in the other room, and all the time you up here in your bedroom, with that — that girl! I never heard such goings on, and your father and mother hardly out of the house. Responsible I am, while they're not here, and I'm not having it! D'you hear? I'm not having it!''

William had gone very white. The music in his room stopped and Carol was just behind him. You could see that they were both absolutely stunned.

''Carol and I have been playing records, Mrs Bartle,'' was what William said in the end.

''In your *bedroom?*'' She was nearly choking.

''It's where I keep the stereo,'' William said. ''I often have friends up here.''

''You mean to tell me that your father and mother let you spend hours on end closeted in your bedroom with *girls? I'll* be bound! There's to be no more carrying-on like this while I'm in charge. Oh no. I've never . . .''

38

On and on she went. It was terrible. None of us had ever heard anything like it. We'd have family rows, all right, but they always had some sense in them. Mum and Dad would never in a million years have gone on like that.

While she was still gasping and spluttering Carol suddenly pushed William aside and ran straight past us and down the landing and past Barty. She was crying. William stood for a minute and then went after her. We heard the front door bang.

In the silence Barty wheezed. I remember hearing the tick of the grandfather clock at the top of the stairs, making the whole thing even weirder. That tick was so familiar, old as the back of my hand, but nothing else was.

"*Now* where've they gone?" Barty said at last. The wind had gone out of her sails.

"Look, Mrs Bartle," I said. "I'm sorry you're upset. But I expect William's pretty upset as well. This was the first time she's ever been round here, and I expect he wanted her to enjoy it."

"And Mummy and Daddy would have let them play music, of course they would!" Lucy piped up. "And even if they were cross with William they wouldn't have said it till she'd gone. It's rude manners."

I honestly thought Barty was going to throw a fit. I was even a bit frightened. It suddenly occurred to me that she might lock William out, like Terence Bratby's aunt did him once when he was back late. She looked mad enough. I couldn't think what had got into her. One minute she was down there munching biscuits and

39

dozing over the telly, and the next she was rampaging and stomping up the stairs like Lady Macbeth or somebody. *Was* she mad? After all, we didn't have any guarantee. Just because she looked after Mum for a time thirty years ago, didn't mean she automatically couldn't be mad. One in ten of the adult population of this country spends part of their life in a mental home. This is a large number.

Her face began to crumple now that there was no one there to shout at. She could hardly shout at Lucy and me.

"Look, why don't you go down and finish watching your programme?" I said. "I'll make a cup of tea and open a tin of soup for you."

"And then could you put me to bed, please, Oliver," Lucy said quick as a flash. Poor kid. She was scared stiff. Even without her reading all those books and having a strong sense of the dramatic, you could hardly expect her to want to be tucked in by Barty after that lot. Not tonight, anyway.

"I'll do you now," I said. "You go down, Barty. Shan't be a minute."

She looked at us for a moment, and she looked so sagging and bewildered that you could hardly believe what had just happened. Then she turned and went off downstairs, lumbering and breathing loudly.

Lucy and I watched her go, then tiptoed into Lucy's room. I don't know why we tiptoed. We shut the door quietly behind us.

"What's the matter with her?" Lucy's eyes go very stretched out and pale when she's scared. "What will she do?"

40

"Don't worry, Albertine," I told her. "Got a bit over-excited watching *Crossroads*, I expect. Ha ha."

You could see that Lucy didn't fall for this.

"The thing is, she isn't used to responsibility, and suddenly realized she didn't know where William was. She keeps forgetting how old we are. I expect she just panicked."

"But she was mad even when she did know. She was *furious*."

"Come on, Albertine. Here's your pyjamas. She'll be right as rain in the morning."

I wasn't about to explain to Lucy what had been going through Barty's dirty old mind. It made *me* feel dirty. Poor old William. His first girl friend. Romeo and Juliet straight down the plughole.

"I haven't got time to read tonight. Got to make the supper. You read it yourself, and if your light's still on when I come up, we'll finish the chapter together."

She just lay there, not a bit lit up like she usually is, even at bedtime.

"They haven't been gone very long at all, have they?" she said. "Mummy and Daddy."

"They'll be back," I told her. "Stout heart. Tin soldier."

"Tin soldier," she repeated.

I gave her a quick hug. Her bones were like a bird's.

" 'Night, Boris," she said. That was her private name for me, don't ask me why.

" 'Night, Albertine."

"Bloody old Barty," I thought, and went down to make the tea.

41

4

Barty didn't lock William out that night. In the end, the boot was on the other foot. She had to wait up for him. Usually, even if she was half-way through a film, she'd switch off the telly at eleven like clockwork. Then she creaked round the house checking the list of switches and locks Mum had left for her, and so to bed. So far, nobody had wanted to stay out after eleven, but as I sat waiting with Barty that night, I could see that there would most likely be another showdown when someone did. It could easily be me — I'm often back later than eleven when I've been round to Nigel's for a group practice. (We were forming a group, called Loose Change.)

I thought how crazy it was that my parents had left instructions for everything under the sun except the things that really mattered. Old Barty knew how often to water the house plants, and where to order the meat, and how many pints of milk we had, and where all the telephone numbers were for doctors and plumbers, and so on. But no one had told her the important things. She hadn't known we were allowed to take friends up to our rooms, and she wouldn't know that William and I were allowed out after eleven as long as we said where we were, and got back by twelve. (After this time there were special arrangments.) I could think of a whole list of other things. She wouldn't know that none of us likes liver, and that Lucy is allowed to stay the night with Louise Skinner if she's invited, and that she can go out alone on her bike as far as Shooters' Corner.

Not only that, but she didn't know anything about us. It suddenly struck me when I was making her soup, that we weren't really a family any more, even if we were in our own house. What really brought this home was seeing the round red biscuit tin. This might not sound very significant, but it was. On Saturday and Sunday mornings we all had tea and biscuits in Mum's and Dad's room. William, Dad and I all took it in turn to get up and make the tea and load the tray. Then we'd all sprawl over everywhere, talking and eating biscuits, and it was one of the best parts of the week, looking back on it. A kind of indoor picnic. Lucy always chose the biscuits to go into the red tin. She'd shut her eyes and pick one out every time as if it was a Lucky Dip, which it wasn't exactly, considering she knew exactly what was in there anyway, and would feel around for the kind she really wanted. We all used to try to get her going, and egg her on to do her impressions, and we usually ended up with some kind of breakfast cabaret.

While the soup was heating up I hid the red tin behind some old storage jars. I suddenly couldn't bear the thought of old Barty rummaging round in it with her little eyes glued on the telly. I thought perhaps I'd see if the others wanted to keep up the weekend tea thing. We easily could, in one of our rooms. It would help to keep

43

the family going.

I was not altogether delighted at sitting out another session of telly with Barty. This one was even more like a wake than the first night. The funny thing was, *I* was keen to stay up until William came back, because I wanted to see how he was, and also give some moral support. But you could also see that Barty, expecially once it got past eleven, was equally keen for me to be there. It was as if she thought I was going to be moral support for *her*.

By half past eleven she had really got cold feet. She kept flicking her eyes towards the clock, and looking sideways at me, but I just went on pretending to be as engrossed as hell in this terrible American movie.

"Should we send for the police, do you think?"

"Sorry? What?"

I'd heard her all right the first time.

"I said the police — did we ought to send for them? Look at the time."

"It's only just gone half eleven. He's nearly sixteen, you know."

She looked back at the screen, and started rustling in her sweet bag again. This really irritated me. If she actually did think William was out there being disembowelled, or something, it was a pretty nonchalant way of reacting.

"Of course, he was in a terrible state when he went out," I remarked. "I hope he hasn't gone and done something silly."

She whipped her head round and looked at me really popeyed then, and it was just bad luck that at that very

44

moment we heard the front door open. I'd really got her worried.

"It's William!" I yelled. I did this so that he'd know straight away that I was up and with him.

He walked in and looked straight at Barty.

"I'd like you to write first thing in the morning to my parents, Mrs Bartle. You have the forwarding address. I would like you to tell them exactly what happened tonight. I shall be writing my own account."

He was brilliant. I really admired old William. Cool as a cucumber, spelling it out. Barty heaved herself out of her chair but didn't look at either him or me.

"You've been out late! Oh, I shall write a letter, never you fear!"

"And what'll you put in it? That Carol and I were up in my room playing records? What else? That's all, isn't it? You know it is. I can play records up there with my friends every night of the week if I want to, if you want to know. Ask them. Go on, write and ask them. You'll see. And thank you very much indeed for ruining—"

He just turned then and rushed out. He was nearly crying.

"Good night, Mrs Bartle," I said and I followed him.

I wasn't sure whether to go along to his room. In the end, I decided not. If I was crying, or nearly crying, I wouldn't want him to see. So in the end I just gave a tap on his door and said, " 'Night, William. Good for you. That told her!" and scooted straight back to my room to save him the embarrassment of not telling me to come in.

I suppose I expected there would be a state of open war from then on, which does show that I tend to be excitable

45

in times of crisis.

Next morning, things seemed different. When I got down old Barty was making breakfast as usual. I went down there prepared for hostilities to commence. The sun was pouring into the kitchen and there was a smell of toast and bacon, and she said,

"Come along, now. It's just ready."

This is a ridiculous thing, and probably a comment on human nature, but it is almost impossible to be hostile to someone who has just given you a plateful of bacon and eggs and fried bread. So I just said, "Thanks very much. Smashing," and sat down, feeling rather a traitor to William all the same.

"Lovely day," she said. "The sun's shining already."

She always did this. Told everybody what the weather was like when they could see it for themselves with their own eyes.

"Give Lucy a shout, will you, dear? They're nearly done."

So I yelled up to Lucy, who called back. I thought that Barty wasn't really so bad. She did scrambled eggs specially for Lucy in the morning, and knew how she liked them, still quite soft and pale and before they go yellow and crumbly.

Lucy came skipping down like a shot.

"Oooh, thanks!"

She sat next to me with one leg tucked up under her as she often does but is not supposed to do at the table. She seemed to have clean forgotten about last night. She didn't even exchange a meaningful look with me, as I'd been quite prepared for. She seemed so light-hearted you'd have almost expected her to be humming. Except that no one can hum with a mouth full of scrambled egg and toast. You can talk with one, though, and she did.

"That's a new dressing gown, isn't it? Isn't it pretty? Is it real quilted silk?"

"Not exactly silk, dear, but it's nice, isn't it? Got it from Marks. Thought I'd treat myself. Had that old candlewick for years."

She had on this long white quilted thing, with pink and green flowers. Bit of a change from her usual black — not that her dressing gown had been that, of course. She'd kept her dressing gown on at breakfast since she'd been with us, and it certainly had been somewhat tatty. Then afterwards, when we'd gone to school, she'd go up and spend ages in her bathroom. (I knew this because Lucy stopped at home one day with a cold.) You could tell that she really enjoyed this aspect of things. Lady of leisure. And now she'd bought this posh toga to make it seem even more luxurious. Once we'd left for school today, she'd wash up, then go upstairs and feel even more luxurious than usual. You couldn't help feeling sorry for someone who has something like this for the highlight of their day.

"It is nice, Barty," I told her. "I like the colours."

"To match the suite, you see."

I couldn't think what on earth she meant. Then it dawned on me. The bath and things in there were pink. That really got me.

William came in, and I said immediately,

"Look, William, Barty's got a new dressing gown."

"Of purest silk," Lucy said, through scrambled egg.

47

"Very nice," he said, and sat down.

"Here's your bacon and egg, dear." She put them down in front of him.

And that was it. War over. The whole thing as good as dead and buried.

It wasn't entirely, of course. We did talk about it, but not until we'd seen Lucy to her school and were walking on to our own.

"You can't blame her all that much," I said. "She's just taking her duties too seriously. She'll settle down. She's just out of touch with our generation."

"You can say that again." He was naturally still somewhat bitter. "What sort of a fool do you think I looked in front of Carol?"

"It was terrible," I agreed.

"And as good as calling her a — a — " He obviously couldn't bring himself to use the word he had in mind — tart, probably.

"She watches too much television," I said. "And what's worse, she believes it. She probably thinks we're all on drugs. She probably goes sniffing round our rooms for hypodermics when we're out."

He didn't laugh at this. It was perhaps a bit early to expect him to take the whole thing lightly.

"Is she coming again tonight?"

"*What?* After that?"

"Well, if not tonight, in a day or two. She must. Like going straight up again in a 'plane. If Mum and Dad were here she'd be able to. And they'll spell it out to old Goosegog, as soon as they get your letter."

He brightened up somewhat.

48

"I've already written it."

He patted his pocket.

"Good. Gordon Bennett! Talk about gooseberries and currant scones!"

He did laugh then.

That evening we had a real break. Mum and Dad rang up.

It was marvellous to hear their voices again — it was five days since they'd last rung, and this would be the last time. It was I who answered the 'phone. In a single instant everything seemed back to normal again, and Barty shrank right down to size. They sounded happy and excited, especially Mum. Lucy had her turn to talk next, and was hopping from one foot to the other the entire time. When it was William's go I admit I held my breath. But as it turned out, he just talked about ordinary things, and then right at the end, quite casually, he said, "By the way, I wonder if you'd just mind having a word with Barty? She's not too clear what the position is about having friends up to our rooms, and staying out at night, and so on."

No one could have passed it off with more careless ease. Barty took over and seemed nervous, and kept saying, "Yes, yes, of course . . ." a lot, and we exchanged triumphant glances. When she came off Lucy had one last turn, and when she put the 'phone down she burst into tears.

"Now now, my lamb, what's all this?" Barty said. She tried to hug Lucy, but she wriggled free and ran to me.

"I want Mummy and Daddy!" The last thing Lucy is is a cry-baby, but as I have said, she does have a very

49

affectionate nature.

"They'll soon be back," I said. "And you've got us."

"They *won't* be back soon!" She stamped her foot. "That's a fib. They'll be gone for yonks and donks, you know they will!" (Yonks and donks is something Lucy once came out with when she was really little. She meant to say "donkey's years" but it came out wrong. We've all used it ever since.)

Mum always said that when Lucy was in a state it was better to let her have a good cry, or yell, or whatever, and get it out of her system, rather than try to coax her out of it. So I took her up to her room and let her do that. But I sat there while she lay curled on the bed. I knew she'd want me to. I looked at the layout on the floor and wondered whatever game she'd been playing. All farms and railways and petrol stations mixed in with forts and Indians, not to mention a gang of little fat Crusaders storming up from behind her doll's house. She certainly did have an imagination.

I am not an expert at writing books, and am not too sure how to get on to the really big event that comes next in the story. It didn't happen for another six weeks. I can't very well give a blow by blow account of everything that happened, even if I could remember. But on the other hand, I think I should try to give a general picture of our lives during that time, or no one will understand just how this event affected us.

In the end we got on all right with old Barty. (The fact that we now sometimes called her "Goosegog" behind her back may or may not prove this. You are supposed only to give nicknames to people you are fond of. I am not that convinced of this. There are two masters at school that everybody hates like poison, and I wouldn't dare even tell you what *their* nicknames are.)

There were never any other rows like the first one, though there was nearly a great fuss kicked up about Lucy and Mr Poynton.

The point about Lucy is that she has a lot of grown-up friends. If anything, she has more of these than friends of her own age. Some of them she picks up right outside the house, where she plays hopscotch on the pavement, or waylays people with popguns or tows a string of trucks along, or whatever. People stop and talk to her, and naturally realize what a character she is, and get friendly. I daresay she's a lot more interesting than some of these people's grown-up friends.

Anyway, you might call this group her "front gate" friends, and there are plenty of them. You can't walk anywhere around here with Lucy without nearly everyone you meet saying "Hello". She has the widest circle of acquaintances of anybody I know.

I must admit that at one stage Mum and Dad did worry a bit about this, and so did I. After all, little kids are not supposed to talk to strangers. But telling this to Lucy was like trying to tell the grass not to grow (which I have tried, incidentally). In the end, we just had to let it go. Naturally we kept a fairly strict eye on her, especially when she was younger, and she sure as hell knew she wasn't to get into any cars with anybody, or go off with them. She knew that all right.

But there were some of these front gate people she met who got to be real friends of hers. They were a pretty mixed bunch. There was Mrs Chick (I ask you!) who was about a hundred and ninety years old and walked with a stick. We actually used to call her Chick the Stick till Lucy got friendly with her, and wouldn't let anybody. She used to go round there and talk to her and play with this collection of cards. Mrs Chick had been collecting every single postcard, Christmas, Birthday, Easter and Valentine card since she was born, from what I could gather. Lucy really enjoyed sorting them about, and she said a lot of them had real lace and ribbon and flowers on, and brought back Mrs Chick's memories.

That is one example of Lucy's friends, and there were quite a few more, including this Mr Poynton. I'm not much good at people's ages, but he was certainly sixty-five because he used to go for his pension. He had a dachshund dog called Spider, which I suppose was meant as a joke. He was certainly that kind of character, which is probably why he and Lucy got on so well. If ever he was not feeling too good Lucy would take this Spider for his walk, though naturally not in the park. And she would go round to his house to talk as well. Whatever they found to talk about was a mystery. *He* didn't have any collection of cards or anything else, from what I could make out. I once or twice tried to find out, but old Lucy just said,

"We just *talk* the same as anybody else, silly!"

You can guess what is coming. The minute old Barty found out that Lucy went to visit Mr Poynton she began to show signs of brewing up to the same kind of blasting that William got. It was one Saturday lunchtime and Lucy was a bit late, *I* knew where she was all right. She'd told me. I don't want to give the impression that my parents were negligent. She knew she had to say where she was going.

"Just stick hers in the oven, I should," I told Barty. "She won't be long. She's just gone to Mr Poynton's."

"Who's he?"

"This old boy who lives in one of the bungalows on Silver Street."

"Old boy? You mean old man?"

"Pretty old," I said, not wanting to sound personal, considering her own age. "Old age pensioner, anyway."

"On her *own*?"

This was when William and I began to see the warning signs.

"With an old man?"

"She often does," I said. "He's a friend of hers."

"And Mum and Dad perfectly approve of the friendship." William was very firm. "He's an old family friend, and Lucy visits him whenever she likes."

"As a matter of fact, she's the light of his life," I said. "He told Mum so."

"Joking, of course," William said.

"Not necessarily," I said. "I can't think who else would be. He hasn't got any daughters, because he's never been married."

The minute I'd said this I could see it was rather tactless. Barb and Janet could hardly be described as the lights of Barty's life. Luckily, she didn't seem to notice. She just said "Not married!" and sniffed, and banged Lucy's dinner plate into the oven in an unnecessary way.

At any rate, the storm was averted. But there would

have been one, all right, if William and I had not nipped it in the bud.

In some ways Barty blossomed out during those weeks. Apart from her flowered toga thing, she actually bought a winter coat that was brown instead of black, and she started going to a hairdresser once a week. Not that this affected us one way or the other, except in the sense that it seemed to make her more pleased with herself, and therefore more pleased with us.

She did not, unfortunately, stop watching television with bags of biscuits and sweets, which made us all outlaws in the evenings. We did once, in a rush of blood to the head, try to get her interested in playing a few games instead. We didn't choose Monopoly or anything too complicated for her. We decided to start her off with Ludo, and work her up to something more interesting. Unfortunately, we forgot to consult the television guide first. If we'd picked a bad night, we might have stood a chance. As it was, we ran straight into *Crossroads* followed by one of those everlasting Quiz games. We stood as much chance as a lump of ice in hell.

But on the good side, she did look after us well in the sense that she cooked good meals, and made sure all our clothes were clean and took me to the doctor when I got crusty eyelids. And she did ask us what we'd done at school that day, even if we didn't feel much like telling, and even if you could see that she was only asking out of kindness, not because she really wanted to know. The point is, she *asked*.

It is no use pretending that she underwent a transformation and became again as she had been in the old gooseberry-picking days, as Mum remembered her. That would not be true. And it is no use pretending that we ever felt really at home with her. We got some letters from Mum and Dad during those first few weeks, but we knew that soon there would be silence. You cannot post letters or make telephone calls in the Amazon jungle. But each time we had one of these letters, it had the same effect on us all. It brought home to us that the three of us were utterly alone, Barty or not. And it made us home-sick, even though we were at home. And the feeling got worse with each letter that came, probably because we knew that soon the absolute silence would begin.

5

It was the end of October when the blow fell. In fact, I may as well be exact, and say that it was Hallowe'en. You may or may not take this as an omen, but I certainly did, and so did the others. It was, as far as we were concerned, the most Meaningful Coincidence of our entire lives.

I ought to explain about coincidences. In our family a lot of them tend to happen, but they happen mainly to me and Lucy. William's theory is that this is because we are both Cancer, and consequently nuts. I am especially interested in the subject, and must now be careful not to bore you with my ideas. As a matter of fact, I keep a special book in which I write down every single coincidence, however small, and on this occasion, October 31st was a red letter entry.

Not another coincidence in my book came up to it. Some of them are trivial, or might seem so — like suddenly finding yourself humming a certain tune, and then switching on the radio and finding that exact tune being played. Some of them are just to do with numbers. Like buying a raffle ticket number 73 in the morning, and then later in the day being given a page to read out loud in class, and *that* being page 73. These may sound nothing, but in fact the odds against it are millions to one, and there was a man called Kammerer who spent practically his whole life collecting these kind of numbers and statistics, and trying to make some kind of pattern out of them. In the end he committed suicide.

But some of these coincidences really *do* seem meaningful. A master at school put me on to Jung, and his Theory of Synchronicity. It is too complicated to go into here, but if you are interested you can find it in his *Collected Works* Volume VIII, *The Structure and Dynamics of the Psyche*. What it amounts to is that there is a lot more to existence than we think, that there are layers and dimensions that we aren't aware of most of the time — sort of "There are more things in heaven and earth, Horatio, than are dreamed of in your philosophy." This quote from *Hamlet* is one I come out with when I'm trying to prove this point, with the result that the minute I start talking about coincidences, everyone calls me Horatio.

But most people, if they are honest, have had instances of Synchronicity in their lives. When I first mentioned it at home, Mum immediately told me how she had met Dad. He had come to live in a house with a garden that ran down to the end of hers. He'd been there over a year and they had never met, for the simple reason that all there was at the end of Mum's garden was this waste ground with the compost heap and bonfire, and she never went down there. Then, one day, she said, she had suddenly had the feeling that, to put it in her words "she would have to cast off the old love before she could find the new." (Like a snake shedding its skin, I suppose

57

she meant.) What this meant was that she knew she had to burn a trunk-load full of love letters that she'd kept, and used to read, from a student she'd once been engaged to. She used to like reading them, she said. They were apparently really good love letters, some of them thirty pages long, and hundreds of them, because he used to write every single day during the vacs. Anyway, she waited for a good still day, because she naturally didn't want a wind blowing these letters all over the neighbours' gardens, then lugged this trunk right down to the bottom of the garden and lit a bonfire.

The next thing she knew, there was Dad looking at her over the fence. He had seen the smoke from the bonfire rising into the air and come down to ask whoever was there if his family could burn some lopped-down trees on the waste ground, because there wasn't room in their garden. Those old love letters had been a smoke signal, she said. She also admitted that if she had read this in some crummy woman's magazine she would have thought it absolute muck, but the fact was that it happened to be true.

I was impressed by this, and put it in my book. It wasn't strictly a coincidence that had happened to me, but it did affect me indirectly, inasmuch as if it hadn't happened, my parents would not have *been* my parents, and I would consequently not be me. Wheels within wheels.

To come back to Hallowe'en. There were two reasons why it was already a meaningful date in our family. The first was that it was at a Hallowe'en Party that Mum and Dad got engaged, and the second was that it had been

Hallowe'en the day we moved into that house. They were quite chuffed about this, and said it was a good sign, though naturally the rest of us were not so impressed. But I do remember we had a bonfire in the garden and carved pumpkin lanterns which looked really weird glowing in the windows because there weren't even any curtains up then. And we wore masks and prowled round the house in the dark, and it was extra spooky with our not knowing the house, and which corners anyone might jump out from.

On this fateful Hallowe'en we had all realized what the date was, but with Mum and Dad not being there, and all of us but Lucy being a bit old for all this now, had decided to skip the party aspect of things, though we did help Lucy to carve a pumpkin. But it did happen to fall on a Saturday. We had secretly re-established our Saturday and Sunday morning tea and biscuits, which we had in William's room as being furthest away from Barty's. (Not that there was any reason why she should stop us doing it. We just didn't want to make her feel an outsider, and also the secrecy was half the fun.)

It was my turn to creep down and make the tea. We usually had it around half seven to eight, because at weekends Barty didn't get up till nine, to give herself a break. We'd told her she needn't get up till eleven, for that matter. I'd set my alarm clock because it was still dark at seven thirty, and I wouldn't necessarily wake up otherwise.

It always seems funny to be the first down on a dark morning when everyone else is asleep and the house dead quiet. That morning it was raining, it was lashing against the black kitchen windows. I remember thinking that jacket potatoes on a bonfire wouldn't stand much chance if that lot kept up. I filled the kettle right up and got the milk and mugs on to a big tray. Then I went to get the red biscuit tin from its hiding-place. This was on the top shelf in the larder, at the back, where only William and I could reach it. It was crammed with gingernuts and chocolate digestives that Lucy had chosen on the way back from school the day before.

I took it into the kitchen. The kettle was singing and now the wind and rain were really rattling against the panes, and it was quite spooky, even though it was morning and not night. I forgot to mention that I was using a torch. With our house being L-shaped, Barty might have looked out of her window and seen if I'd turned the light on.

Then I heard something else. It was quite a long way off and was a noise I'd never heard before. It was horrible. It was like someone having a truly terrible asthma attack, and groaning at the same time. I knew it wasn't Lucy having me on. She can do impressions all right, but not like that. Just then the kettle came to the boil and switched itself off, and there was a lull in the rainstorm and I heard it again, clearly. Only this time it was louder, and coming nearer, and I could hear a creaking tread. Barty was coming downstairs. It sounds crazy now, but I grabbed the red biscuit tin and rammed it into a saucepan cupboard.

I whipped round to face the door, like a thief caught red-handed, but it never opened. What I heard then was a terrible sawing noise in someone's throat, and then a deep, rough gurgling, and I knew then that it was Barty, and that she was dying.

I was in the hall and switched on the light and there she was. She was sprawled on her back half-way down the stairs, her flowered toga right up above her knees, and little rattling noises were still coming from her throat.

I think I went slowly to the bottom of the stairs. I think I knew it was too late to hurry. I went up three stairs, to the stair below her pink fur slippers. The rattling had nearly stopped. There was just a faint whisper of breath. I craned forward and saw that her eyes were wide open, looking right up. I yelped then. I couldn't help it. I stopped myself immediately. I took a hard grip on myself.

"Barty!" It didn't come out very loud, so I said it again — "Barty!" — and this time it came out as a shout.

She lay absolutely still now. She was never going to move again. Dead.

I don't know how long I stood there, and there's no point in knowing, because there was nothing I could have done. All I know is I stood there long enough for that picture of her with her white veiny legs and wide-open mouth and eyes, and rumpled roses dressing gown to be there for me for ever. If I closed my eyes, I could see it now.

My first thoughts were all mixed up. I knew that I had to tell somebody, somebody grown up. And I even remember thinking it was terribly funny that Mum had wanted someone grown up to be there in case something

61

awful happened, and now it had, and that very person was the last in the world who could help now. I thought perhaps I should dial 999 and then thought perhaps it should be the doctor. I wanted to ask William, but I couldn't. There was nothing, absolutely nothing, that would make me edge past or stride over that body. I could have done it, but I wouldn't.

I went back down the few stairs away from it. I was shaking. I admit it. I thought of yelling to William, yelling so loud he'd be bound to wake up, even though he was so far off. But two things stopped me. The thought of yelling over somebody who had just that minute died, seemed absolutely wrong. I could never have brought myself to do it. I don't know a lot about sacrilege, but I'm sure it would have been. The other thing was Lucy. Her room was the nearest, the first along that landing, and she was often the first to wake up anyway. Even now I had the terrible thought that she might suddenly come skipping to the top of the stairs in her pyjamas (she starts skipping the minute she wakes up) and even start hopping down the stairs, and then see *that*.

It was this that got me into action. I had to cover the body over. That was the first thing. My mind was so muzzy at first that I couldn't think what to use. I even thought of taking down a curtain. Then I remembered the cupboard under the stairs. I went in there and got the first rug I could see. It was a furry car rug, a kind of mock leopard skin, and terrible as it sounds I nearly giggled. Corpses are meant to be draped in white, not in furry mock leopard, though it did cross my mind that Barty herself might quite have liked it. She had once remarked on how beautiful it was, and stopped Lucy from taking it into the garden, saying it was too expensive.

It was awful actually doing it. To be truthful, I went up the three stairs and then half shut my eyes and leaned slightly forward and threw it up, holding the bottom corners. When I looked, I could see that it had covered her face, and I was so relieved that I wouldn't have to drag it back and try again, that her slithering down caught me right off balance, and I yelled, really yelled this time, and stumbled and fell on to the hall floor.

I scrambled up. Barty was even more sprawled than ever now. One of her slippers had come off. You could see the yellowy sole of her foot and half her leg sticking from under the rug. And her face had come uncovered. I was in a blue funk.

"Oliver! Hello!"

Lucy was at the top of the stairs and I acted quicker than I'd ever acted in my life. I leapt on to the stairs and yanked the rug up to cover the face. I pulled it really high, to make sure, and then I carried on to the top. Don't ask me how. I truthfully don't remember.

"What? What is it? What's Barty doing? Is she hurt?"

I was shaking like a jelly. I dragged Lucy along the landing and yelled,

"William! Quick!"

"What's *happened?*" Lucy screamed. She tried to break free but I hung on to her wrists.

"It's all right," I said. "It's all right."

The funny thing is, I didn't so much say it, as hear myself say it, as if I were someone else. It was a pretty crazy thing to say, anyway. It *wasn't* all right.

"It's not, it's not! Let go, you pig!"

"Listen, Lucy, you're not to go down there. Barty's — well, she's had an accident."

"Has she fallen downstairs? Is she hurt?"

"Lucy. She didn't exactly fall down. She — I think she had a heart attack."

She left off struggling.

"She's *dead!*"

"Yes."

Her voice went up in an awful, eerie, high-pitched wail. She started to cry.

"William!" I yelled again.

His door opened and there he was and he could tell something was really wrong.

"You'll have to telephone! You'll have to get the doctor. Barty's dead."

"Dead? What d'you mean?"

"*Dead* you fool! She's down at the bottom of the stairs. I heard her — it was a heart attack. Look, use the 'phone in Mum and Dad's room. But get a doctor, will you?"

He came slowly up and then past us and stood looking down the stairs.

"God!"

He stood for a minute, then crossed to the other landing. I towed Lucy along with me after him, quickly, so's she wouldn't have time to look down the stairs. She did, though. But she didn't scream or anything.

We all stood round the 'phone at the bedside and the same thought struck us all at the same time.

"We don't know his number!" It was William who actually said it. The 'phone in there was only an extension in case someone rang at night or something. There was no directory and no list of numbers.

"We could dial nine nine nine," I said.

I didn't want to have to pass that body again. I didn't want anybody to have to. And if William did, he'd have to do it on his own. Lucy couldn't possibly, and I'd have to stay with her.

"Hang on." Even his voice was trembling. "I'll ring Steve. Then he can give me the number."

I told you William was cool and calm in an emergency. It would have taken me a hundred years to think of that.

So he dialled this friend of his. He obviously got through to Steve's mother and had to start off by apologizing for disturbing her so early.

"The thing is, Mrs May, we really badly need Dr Warden's 'phone number. This Mrs Bartle who was staying with us has had — well, she's dead, I'm afraid. She's lying on the stairs, dead, and we're up in Mum's room, and — "

I could hear all these excited noises at the other end of the line, and William kept saying, "No, we're all right, honestly. If you could just give me Dr Warden's number."

In the end he got it and repeated it twice to be sure to remember it. There wasn't a pad or pencil. The minute he put the receiver down he picked it up again and dialled the number. Lucy and I kept dead quiet. I was repeating the number over and over in my head, in case he'd got it wrong, and I think Lucy was doing the same.

The 'phone call only took a minute.

"He said five minutes," William said. "Give him five minutes."

Then another thought struck us all at the same time. This time it was me who said it.

"Someone'll have to go down and let him in."

Lucy was crying again, very softly, and I put my arm round her.

"I'll go and get my dressing gown," William said.

"I don't mind going." I was lying.

"I'm the oldest. You stop with Lucy. You'd better get your dressing gowns on as well. It doesn't feel as if the heating's come on. Barty must have forgotten to set the control switch last night."

It sounded weird to hear him refer to her. Because she *wasn't* any more.

We all went back, past the top of the stairs and the heap at the bottom. I went into Lucy's room and got her dressing gown and then took her along to my room while I got mine. William came in.

"I think I'll wait till I actually hear the bell ring," he said.

"Good idea."

I knew exactly how his mind was working. I hadn't been able to get past that body myself, in cold blood. I only did it when I had to. Once the doctor was actually there, at the door, William would be able to do it. We sat huddled on my bed.

"I was just making the tea," I said. "I'd just laid the tray and everything. In fact the kettle had just boiled."

"Did you hear her then?"

"I didn't know what it was at first. I didn't hear her fall, only those awful — moans." I wasn't going to go into details now, not in front of Lucy. "I don't think she fell downstairs, just collapsed when she was nearly down."

"Gordon Bennett! It must've been awful."

"It can't have been my fault. I mean, she can't have come down because she saw a light. I was using the torch."

"Don't be a fool. If people are going to have a heart attack, they have one. Of course it wasn't anybody's fault."

"Though she might've seen the torch, and thought it was a burglar."

"Look, if she was looking out through her curtains at half past seven, which would need to be a miracle, and had by chance seen a torch, she'd have gone along the landing to Mum's room, and dialled nine nine nine."

Lucy was very quiet. I hoped it didn't mean she was suffering from shock. I could hardly have just changed the subject to something cheerful, though. When the doorbell rang we all jumped. William got up quickly and went out without a word. I tightened my grip round Lucy, because I knew her. She was thinking of William getting past that body as well.

I can't describe the relief when I heard Dr Warden's voice in the hall. It was like surfacing after being suffocated in a nightmare. He sounded very business-like and his voice was quite loud. He wasn't talking in hushed tones as we had been up to now. After a bit, we heard William call up.

"All right, you two. You can come down now."

I took Lucy's hand and we went down.

"Come along, you two." Dr Warden was standing at the foot of the stairs. "Hello, Lucy. I should get into the kitchen, if I were you. I've just asked William if there's a cup of tea going."

"I was just making one," I said. "The kettle had just boiled." (Though heaven knew how long ago that had been. I didn't.)

He had moved her on to the hall floor, clear of the stairs, and she was completely covered now. I was glad. I didn't want Lucy to see even a foot sticking out.

"There's a good girl." He patted Lucy's head as we went past. "Just give me five minutes, will you, and I'll be with you. Terrible morning. All do with a good strong cup of tea."

We went towards the kitchen.

"Plenty of sugar!" he called after us. "All of you."

I knew what that meant. Shock. He thought we were all in shock. I suppose we were, if it comes to that.

William had switched the kettle on and it was already boiling again. I looked at the tray I'd set out, and the round red biscuit tin. It seemed a hundred years since I last saw them.

William got an extra cup and saucer and I moved things from the tray on to the table. We weren't talking. I think we were all thinking of Dr Warden, and what he was doing out there in the hall. I was, anyway.

The tea looked very brown. William put two big teaspoons of sugar in all the cups.

"I don't think I want a biscuit," Lucy said.

I looked at the red tin and thought that I would get rid of it later. I'd put it in the dustbin. We'd have to start all over with a new tin. Lucy could go and choose one that she liked. A different colour would be best. Green. Or gold. Or blue.

Dr Warden came in and shut the door behind him.

"Ah! Just the job!"

He didn't sit down, just stood there, gulping it. We watched him.

"Got some sugar in! Now. The telephone. One or two calls I'll have to make."

"In the study," William told him. "The door just by where — "

"Ah. Right. Good." He looked at us all hard then, one by one.

"Quite a mess for you, isn't it? Your parents still anywhere where you can get in touch?"

William shook his head.

"Haven't heard for ages. Don't know when we will, now."

The doctor made tut-tutting sounds.

"Grandparents? Aunts and Uncles?"

"No." William said. "Nobody. That's the whole point. That's why Mum got old — got Mrs Bartle in."

"Ah. Yes, I see. So no relations at all, cousins or anything?"

"No. Both my parents were onlys. We — "

"Mrs Bartle, I mean. Next of kin."

"Oh. Yes. Well, two that we know of. She's got two married daughters."

"Know where to contact them?"

69

William thought for a minute then said slowly, "I suppose . . ."

"We'll have to go to her room and look," I said. "Their addresses will be there somewhere. They're both on the 'phone."

"Good. Good. I'll leave it to you, then."

We sat and drank our tea.

"Dr Warden," I said, "was it a heart attack?"

"It was. Not entirely a surprise — to me at any rate."

"Did you *know* she was going to have one?" I was amazed.

He half shrugged.

"It was on the cards. And I warned her about her weight each time I saw her."

"We didn't know she'd been seeing you," William said.

"Oh yes. *Did* she make any effort to diet, do you know?"

I had this picture of old Barty sitting there night after night with her sweets and biscuits, and opened my mouth to answer. Then I had a second picture of how I'd seen her on the stairs.

"Not exactly," I said. "But I don't think she'd have got any fatter."

"Are you sure you can dig out those next of kin?" he asked William. "As soon as you can, really."

"I'll help." I said. It was going to be weird in Barty's room, opening her handbag, perhaps, and looking in drawers. None of us had ever gone in there since she'd moved in.

"Dr Warden . . . " Lucy's voice was very small.

"Yes, Lucy?"

"How long . . . when will . . . will we be left alone with her?"

It had probably been at the back of all our minds. As long as Dr Warden was there, things seemed normal. I didn't want to hear the front door bang behind him and us left with what was under the leopard-skin rug.

"Don't you worry, Lucy. You're going to stop in here like a brave girl, while I go and make a couple of 'phone calls. And then it will be less than an hour, I promise you. Got a radio in here, have you?"

"Yes."

"Well, just you switch that on, and listen to Children's Choice or whatever it is at this time on a Saturday. Any neighbour who could pop in, William?"

"Mrs Fowles next door *would*," William said. "We're not all that friendly, but she would."

"I think she'd better," Dr Warden said. "Want to nip round now, while I make these 'phone calls?"

I sat with Lucy and listened to the radio while William went up to get dressed. In five minutes he was back with Mrs Fowles. I've never liked her all that much, but she was one more live person in the house, one more familiar voice, and it made things better. Besides, you could see that she was upset and worried about us. She kept saying "Oh, you poor dears, what a terrible thing to happen!" And oddly enough, the more she said it was terrible, the better it made me feel. She offered to make us some breakfast, but none of us wanted any.

Dr Warden had a word with her in the hall, but we couldn't hear what they were saying. Then he came back

71

into the kitchen, and said, "I'm going to look in again later. Make sure you've got hold of those daughters of hers. Even one of them will do. Right?"

"Right," we said.

Half an hour later the front door bell rang. Mrs Fowles told us to stop where we were. She went out and closed the door behind her. We heard men's voices, and various noises, and then the front door closed. Mrs Fowles came back in.

"That's done, then," she said. "She's gone."

6

Mrs Fowles took Lucy back next door with her, once she'd dressed.

"I don't *want* to go!" Lucy whispered at me as I got together one or two of her books and things to take. "Why can't I go to Mrs Chick?"

"We need you right next door," I told her. "It's going to be a pretty frantic day. William and I've got a lot to do."

She seemed to understand, and went off quietly enough. The minute she'd gone William and I went up to Barty's room. We could talk more freely with Lucy out of the way.

"God, it was *awful*," I told him. "These terrible groans and wheezes, and at the end there really was a rattling in her throat."

"God."

"And her eyes were wide open."

We stood just inside Barty's room and looked round. The bedcovers were all dragged aside and trailing on the floor. The curtains were still drawn and the bedside light was on.

"Better open the curtains."

We did, and that made it seem better. There's some-

73

thing depressing about drawn curtains in daylight.

"There's her handbag."

It was lying on a velvet armchair. The clothes she'd worn the day before were lying folded by it.

We both sat on the floor (we knew we couldn't sit on the bed) and William tipped the bag out. You could see at a glance that we hadn't struck lucky. There was hardly anything there at all. There was a little toilet bag and some tissues, and keys, a bag of sweets, a spectacle case and a tube of indigestion tablets. We put the stuff back in the bag.

William opened one of the wardrobes. It looked bare. She didn't really have many clothes.

"Bedside drawer."

That was where we found it. She'd obviously kept that drawer for her private things. There was her pension book and savings book and some photos. We didn't really look at them, but they were of her and her family, some of them going back years. Then there was the address book. Barb lived in Birmingham, we knew that. We didn't know her surname, so we went right through the book. There weren't many entries at all, and none of them was Birmingham.

"I've just thought," I said. "You don't put your own family's addresses in books. You know them. You only write addresses you might forget."

"Gordon Bennett. You're right."

"Letters!" I remembered. "She must've kept those. And she's definitely had at least two since she's been here."

We found it. It was from Barb. I really breathed a sigh

74

of relief when I saw that it was headed notepaper printed with the address and 'phone number in blue.

"Right!" William said. "Here we go."

The 'phone call seemed to go on for ages. I tried to hear what Barb was saying at the other end, but couldn't, and couldn't always guess from what William said.

"Strewth! What a woman!"

"What did she say? Is she coming?"

"She's coming, all right. But she's just about got to reorganize the entire universe first. What about the children? What about the new three piece suite she's expecting delivered this afternoon? What about — you'd have thought Barty'd picked a Saturday to snuff it just to annoy *her!*"

"Wasn't she *sorry?*" I was shocked. "Did she cry?"

"Nope. I dunno."

I looked round Barty's room, and for the first time *I* felt like crying.

"Let's go down."

"They'll sort through her things, I expect," William said. "I expect they'll take them all away."

"Is the other one coming? Janet?"

"I expect so. I hope to heaven she's better than *that* one sounds."

We went back to the kitchen and cleared the tea things and then made some coffee. Just as we were doing it, Dr Warden came back, and we gave him some. William gave him Barb's name and address and told him that she'd be down later in the day, and probably Janet as well.

"Are you going to be all right until then? Can't you get

someone in?''

"Lucy's all right," William said. "She's gone next door. And we don't really know anyone all that well — not grownups, I mean. And it being Saturday . . . '

It was true. On Saturday people are always doing things, especially families. They're doing the weekend shopping, or going skating, or to swimming, or piano lessons, or football. People don't want their weekends messed up with other people's deaths. Barb hadn't even wanted hers messed up with her own *mother's*.

Dr Warden asked us to tell Barb to ring him when she arrived, and then he went.

"We ought to go and do some shopping," William said. "I expect we'll have to offer them something."

"We'll get some chips for lunch," I said. "Then we can hook old Lucy back for them. She won't want to stop at the Fowles' for long."

"OK. God, what a mess!"

"Will they stick around till after the funeral?" I asked. "Barb and Sid, I mean." (Sid was Barb's husband.)

"Sidney."

"What d'you mean?"

"What she kept calling him. Over the 'phone. Sidney this and Sidney that."

"Oh. Well, will they?"

"Probably. That'll make it about next Wednesday, I should think."

"Will there be an inquest or a post mortem?"

"No. Dr Warden told me not. Something to do with him having treated her regularly for the condition she died of."

By now I did have an urge to get out of the house. So we had a quick scan round to see what food there was. Barty had already got a big piece of beef in the fridge for Sunday, and some cooked ham. She always gave us cooked ham for Saturday teatime.

"We'll get some more veg," William said. "And bread. And cakes — plenty. If they're anything like her, we can fill 'em up with biscuits."

Going round the local shops was weird that day. In fact, even being on the street was, especially when you passed people you recognized or knew casually. You felt like telling everyone. Like saying, "Listen — Barty's dead!" It didn't seem right for everything to be going on just the same, just an ordinary Saturday morning, when someone's life had just ended. I could see that it was ridiculous to feel like that — after all, they didn't even *know* Barty, and I suppose that among those crowds there was even someone else whose father or mother or relative had died that day. By the law of averages. But it was how I did feel, and I couldn't help it. I even mentioned it to William, and he said, "What do you expect them to do? Have two minutes' silence, or something?" And I wished I had kept quiet. But then a few minutes later he said, "Mmm. I see what you mean."

So he felt it too. Death is too big a thing to take lightly. It's the most enormous thing there is. So it wasn't all that unnatural that I should feel like shouting it out loud to everyone. The only thing was, I couldn't. There was nothing at all you could do. Absolutely nothing.

Going back to the empty house was weird too. Barty had always been in — not just at mealtimes, but all the time. If ever she went out, it was only shopping, while we were at school.

I went round and fetched Lucy and we had our fish and chips, and after that there seemed a blank that we didn't know how to fill. We had to wait in for Barb and Sid. It had started to rain again, so we couldn't even go and kick a ball around. Nobody actually admitted it, but none of us wanted to go up to our separate rooms. I racked my brains. We couldn't play anything too rowdy, out of respect. We couldn't even carve the pumpkin now. After all, Hallowe'en is the night when spirits are supposed to walk abroad, and even if I weren't actually too convinced of this myself, it seemed better not to have Lucy thinking about it. In any case, a lit-up pumpkin would look too much like festivity, and be tactless to Barty's relations. In the end, I suggested Monopoly. It's the kind of game that keeps you occupied, and when we play it, any row we make is in the form of arguments, not laughing.

We'd just got to the stage of putting up hotels when they arrived. We heard the car on the gravel and we all rushed to the window. We were in my room, so we were looking down directly on them and they didn't see us.

He got out first. He had ginger hair flattened down, and a moustache. He went round and opened the passenger door and this woman got out.

"Gordon Bennett! Look at that!"

Barb was a bit of a shock, to put it mildly. I suppose we'd all expected a younger version of Barty. But Barb looked as if she was togged up for a Glamorous Mother of Two contest. She was all in a sort of turquoise, with a matching hat and you could see yellowish curls under it. Not for long, mind. She tottered smartly towards the porch on her stilettos, presumably terrified of getting her outfit wet. We all made a dash for the stairs. William opened the door.

"Mrs — er — I'm afraid we don't actually know your surname . . .?"

"Dark," came the voice. "Oh, what a dreadful day! Do hurry, darling!"

"I'm William Saxon. Please come in."

"Oh, thank you ever so much. And this is my husband, Mr Dark."

"How d'you do, Mr Dark?"

"Oh — well as can be expected. Mustn't complain."

The door closed behind them and Lucy and I went forward. William did all the introductions.

Lucy was probably trying not to stare, because she is always being told off for this, but she was pop-eyed all the same. (As a matter of fact, I don't see why little kids aren't supposed to stare. I don't see how they can ever learn anything if they don't.) Barb probably wasn't what she expected, either. She sure as hell wasn't any archetypal mother figure.

The trouble was, she tried to act as if she was. To be exact, she wasn't so much motherly as bossy, once she'd got dug in — and that didn't take long. We made some tea and took it into the sitting room on a tray, because the way Barb was dolled up she looked as if she expected to be in there. She wasn't exactly dressed for the kitchen.

While we were drinking the tea, Barb was making social conversation.

79

"Nice house," she said. "Isn't it, Sidney?"

"Very nice," he said.

"And I like this dralon suite. The suite that I'm having delivered this afternoon's a sort of dusty pink dralon, isn't it, Sidney?"

"Yes," he said.

"And look — the television's exactly the same model as ours!"

She said what a coincidence it was, wasn't it, Sidney, but it wasn't as far as I was concerned, and it certainly wasn't going down as one in my book. *Millions* of people have got the same TV sets, for heaven's sake. It stands to reason. Jung certainly wouldn't have been impressed.

Off she went about something else. "Isn't it, Sidney?" and he said "Yes" (naturally) and that's more or less how it went on. They were a bit like a pair out of one of those crummy TV so-called comedies that Barty was always watching. Perhaps if people watch that kind of stuff often enough, they get like it.

She didn't even mention her mother, at least to begin with. Nobody who walked in and listened would have known that somebody's mother had just died. All right, so Barb was grown up and had children of her own, but Barty was still her mother and had brought her up, and you would have thought it would have been some kind of a blow to her. But on she rabbited about this and that, while poor old Sidney nodded and said "Yes." I began to hate Barb.

She got into the bossy stage as soon as we'd had the tea and she began to get her bearings.

"Now, will one of you children show us the room

where we shall be sleeping?" she said, plonking down her cup and saucer.

This remark was a bombshell. The thought that they would actually be staying in the house had never even crossed our minds — though I suppose it should have done. It was just that we were so used to leaving those sort of arrangements to grown ups. William fielded the bomb neatly, I thought.

"If you'd like to come up, I'll show you," he said.

Lucy and I goggled at each other. My first thought was that I hoped he wasn't going to put them in Mum's and Dad's room, because I didn't think I could stand that. I needn't have worried. Lucy and I went up after them, and he had taken them along to Barty's room.

"I thought it better to leave things exactly as they were," we heard him saying. "We thought you would want to pack her belongings yourself."

That was good thinking. I told you William was cool in times of crisis. They wouldn't know that we hadn't even thought about it, though, to be honest, I wouldn't have cared all that much if they had. I should think it would be fairly difficult to hurt Barb's feelings. Probably the best way of doing this would be to criticize her hairstyle.

"What a delightful room," we heard her say. "Isn't it, Sidney?"

You can guess what he said. Lucy poked me and began to giggle, but I personally did not think it all that funny. The bed was lying all crumpled, just as Barty had left it that morning, and you would at least have thought that seeing it would have affected her. After all, it had affected William and me, and she wasn't even our mother. I got to thinking about this, later. I've read about people who stuff themselves with sweets and biscuits because they don't get enough love. Usually this is people whose parents don't love them enough. But I got to wondering whether it would work the other way round, and parents could stuff themselves because their children didn't love them enough. I don't see why not. And if so, you could almost say it was Barb's and Janet's fault that old Barty died. After all, she wasn't that old, and the doctor did say it was mostly overweight that had done it. I am not trying to make them out as murderers, or anything. But it's just a thought I'm mentioning, for what it's worth.

I told Lucy to make her bed and tidy up her room, because given half a chance she'd get a real attack of the giggles, which would probably be out of sheer nervousness, but wouldn't look too good, all the same. I went back to my room to do the same, and I could hear Barb saying what a lovely coat, and nearly brand new, too. Poor old Barty.

Don't ask me how we got through the rest of the day. There are some days you remember just with a vague feeling of awfulness, with only a few details. In any case, you sure as hell wouldn't want to hear a blow by blow account of Barb's conversation. Because that much I do remember. She did most of the talking. The minute she'd taken possession of Barty's room and had her suitcase brought up, she began to run everything and everybody. She kept calling us "children".

"Come along, children, tea's on the table", and "Have you washed your hands, children?"

Washed our hands! I ask you! Daft bat. I pitied *her* children, I really did. She'd left them with a neighbour, apparently. She hadn't brought them with her because she thought funerals were morbid, she said. She rang them up later, to check up on them, and she didn't exactly ask them if they'd washed their hands, but she damn nearly did. Then she rang Janet. I managed to hear quite a bit of that as well. From what I could gather, Barb was the bossy one, which meant (I thought at the time) that with any luck Janet would turn out to be better. Little did I know.

"I told her there wasn't the least point in her coming until Monday," she said afterwards. "Given that we can have the funeral on Tuesday. She's only got the one child, you know, but she won't leave him, that I am certain of. She'll bring him, morbid or no morbid."

"How old is he?" I asked.

"Oh — goodness knows. Nine, is he, Sidney. Ten?"

"Yes, dear."

I felt like asking her how morbid she thought it was for Lucy, who was only seven. I mean, it wasn't just a matter of funerals. Poor old Lucy had actually seen that shape under a leopard-skin rug. I didn't exactly ask Barb this, but I felt pretty fed up and murderous, so I did try to needle her a bit.

"It was really horrible this morning," I said.

"What do you mean?" she asked, giving me a funny look.

"Old Ba — your mother — actually — you know . . . " I already began to wish I'd kept quiet.

"Whatever do you mean?" She really snapped it out.

83

"Well — I was in the kitchen, you know, and heard her on the stairs, and the groans and that, and then I had to go out and — "

"I'd rather not hear!"

I'd expected a reaction, but not quite so quickly, and certainly not so strong. Her eyes were bulging and she had a bright red spot on each cheek and her neck was red as well. It must have been a nervous rash, and I almost began to feel sorry for her.

"I don't want to hear another word! And I hope there'll be none of that morbid talk when Janet gets here. Stephen is a sensitive boy, and mustn't be upset."

I was now back to wanting to kill her. Just then somebody let off a fire cracker in the front garden. Some fool confusing Hallowe'en with Guy Fawkes. We jumped nearly out of our skins.

"What's that?"

"Just a banger. Firework. It's Hallowe'en tonight."

"Hallowe'en?"

"When spirits walk abroad — all the souls who have died . . ."

That really did it. She gave me a murderous look and snapped, "Where's your sister? It's time she was in bed."

"Lucy doesn't go to bed till half past eight at weekends," I told her. "It's not even seven yet."

"Seven years old, seven to bed," she chanted, like some frowsty parrot.

I supposed she believed eight years old, eight to bed, and so forth. I expect she really did, though I didn't bother to ask her. I was tempted, mind. I felt like asking her if three in the morning would be all right for William — three forty five, really, because he was fifteen and three quarters. Anyway, it didn't matter that much. Lucy could go to bed, and we'd read. We'd be only too thankful to be out of her way.

"Lucy!" She went into the hall and screeched up the stairs. Her voice really went through you. "You be getting changed and I'll come up and run your bath!"

"Oh, I'll do that!" I said quickly.

I might as well not have spoken. While Barb was running the bath I went into Lucy's room.

"It's not even seven o'clock yet!" She gets very indignant when she thinks she's not being treated in a grown-up way. She really stands on her rights. You can't blame her. I don't remember all that well what it's like to be seven, but I'm pretty sure that if you are, it seems quite a lot to you, and you don't like being treated like a five-year-old or an idiot.

"She's bats," I told Lucy. "Marbleless. When you're in bed, we'll read."

"The Legend of King Arthur?"

"If you like, yes."

She chirped up then. I picked up her pyjamas and she trotted along to the bathroom.

"Come along now, Lucy, the water's just right. Why — whatever? You haven't a stitch on! Where's your dressing gown?"

Lucy was already hopping into the bath.

"Not worth it. Not cold."

The scene that followed is not easy to describe, though probably Dickens would have managed it. Barb was

85

obviously meaning to bath Lucy, actually soap her and stuff, like a baby. The minute Lucy realized this, she went into one of her furies. Old Lucy has a temper like nobody I know. She practically spits. And she was going through a funny stage about baths. Some nights she wouldn't let anyone in there, not even Mum or me. So we let her get on with it.

"Come along, now," I heard Barb say. "Auntie Barbie's going to give you a nice soap."

That did it.

"You're *not* my auntie!" Lucy screamed. "You're not, you're not, you're *not!*"

Then this almighty splash, and a scream, and next minute Barb came rushing out on to the landing. She nearly trampled right over me. Her hair and face were dripping, and her turquoise suit was splattered all over. Lucy must really have slapped her a basinful.

I tried not to laugh, I honestly did, but it was no good. I laughed practically right in her face.

The balloon went up. I forget half she said, but certainly one thing was that she didn't know how her poor mother had coped at her age, and that we were all thoroughly out of hand, and the worst-mannered lot she had ever met, etcetera etcetera. She didn't exactly say that it must have been us that killed old Barty, but as near as dammit she did. And all the time she was shrieking, Lucy was yelling and splashing away on the other side of the door, flailing her arms like a windmill, I guessed, and soaking the whole shop. Barb stopped to draw breath, and just then old Lucy screamed,

"Silly old cow!"

Now that sounds terrible, I know, especially from a seven-year-old. But I can honestly say that I had never heard Lucy say that before. I didn't even know that she *knew* the expression. She didn't get it off me, because I watch what I say when I'm with her, knowing how quick she is to pick things up. But it did sound terrible, I admit it. The only excuse I can think of is that saying it was the only way for her to let off her feelings about Barb. She didn't know anything else strong enough. I couldn't help agreeing. If there actually *is* such a thing as a silly old cow among human beings, then Barb sure as hell was it.

And let's face it, she could have said something far worse. Good old Lucy.

7

It was ages before I got to sleep that night. I had a lot of thoughts and saw a lot of pictures. By this I mean that it was rather like a drowning man seeing his life flash before his eyes. (If, of course, that theory is true. I shouldn't have thought you could prove it. *Nearly* drowning is not the same as drowning.) I am not sure how to describe it, or even whether I ought to try. I think it would be good for me to try, because after all I had had a very unusual experience that morning, one that some people might never have in a whole lifetime.

On the other hand, I can quite believe that some readers might want to skip this. It will not matter if they do. *All* books have skippable pages, even the best. And I'm the world's greatest skipper myself.

What I kept seeing was a series of pictures, like stills from a movie. And they were all of the same thing. Barty. It was not just Barty lying sprawled on the stairs, though there were plenty of those, and in a queer detail that I don't actually remember noticing at the time. My brain must have photographed them without my knowing. I could see some little metal rollers wound in her hair, for instance, one of them half pulled out. And the soles of her feet, crinkled and yellowing, and, most of all, her mouth sagging open. Her mouth seemed to zoom up big enough to swallow me.

And mixed in with this kaleidoscope were pictures of Barty in her old candlewick dressing gown, and her sitting in the big blue armchair with her eyes on the telly and her hand in the chocolate box. And then her ladling out one of her special puddings, very pleased with herself, and, what was really weird, her when she was younger and at her own house. (I must have got this from her photo album, but, there again, I didn't register it at the time.)

And then I got to thinking about her whole life, and whether she had been happy. My own opinion was that she had not, but all that really means is that I personally would not have been happy in her place. She might have been. It is very difficult to judge other people's happiness.

I remembered that she had given Mum a golden childhood, and that cheered me up a bit. But my thoughts and the pictures went round in circles, and they always came back to that sprawled body and open mouth, and I was pretty depressed. In the end I cried. I admit it.

Then I went to sleep, and it was Sunday, and the real nightmare began. Even after all this time I get a definite shrivelling feeling in my stomach when I remember it. It began with a 'phone call from Dr Warden. Barb answered it, which was just like her cheek, to start answering our 'phone before she'd been in the house five minutes. We all knew who it was, because she was calling him by his name the whole time: "Yes, Dr Warden," and "Oh, I do agree, Dr Warden," and so on.

Really sucking up.

We all thought it would be to do with Barty and the funeral arrangements, so we didn't bother listening all that much. When she finally put the 'phone down she looked excited. Those bright red spots were there again, and she called for Sidney and the two of them closeted themselves in the study.

I didn't exactly eavesdrop, just hung around in the hall. Naturally, Barb did most of the talking.

"I told him there was no question of it," I heard her say. "We have no responsibility at all in the matter. When we leave here after the funeral, that's the end of the affair, so far as we're concerned."

"Thank heaven for that," I thought. I lost interest and went upstairs, but after only a couple of minutes she was at the bottom of the stairs screeching for us all to come.

"Dr Warden has asked me to speak to you," she said, obviously bursting with whatever it was. "He didn't want it to be too much of a shock when the social worker arrives. So I said I'd break it to you."

"I'm afraid I don't quite follow," William said.

"Dr Warden has been in touch with the local Council. They're sending round a social worker. Later today, he says."

"Whatever for?" I asked. I thought she'd gone completely bananas, I honestly did.

"To see what's to be done with you all, of course. You never thought you were going to stop here by yourselves for months on end?"

"Our parents didn't want us to, no," William said. "That's why they got Bar — your mother in. But now there's not much alternative."

"It'll be fun," Lucy said. "Like in a book."

"If you think they'll let you stop here all by your-selves," said Barb, "you're mistaken."

"Who's 'they'?" I wanted to know.

"The authorities, of course." She was getting snappy now. "There's rules and regulations about that sort of thing."

"We'll see," William said. It's amazing, looking back, that even then we didn't realize what was going to happen. We really did think we could carry on as we were until Mum and Dad got back.

"It's a free country," I said, when Barb had gone. "And this is our own house. No one can make us do anything we don't want to."

Famous last words.

We had the roast beef before the social worker arrived, and it was a good thing, because afterwards nobody could have eaten a thing. (The beef was overdone, of course — Barb was exactly the type who would over-cook beef. I expect she thought she was getting rid of germs, or something.) The man's name was Mr Parrish — Ken Parrish, he said. He was fairly young, but worried-looking, with ginger hair and beard and very light blue eyes.

To begin with, he asked us all kinds of questions about the family and our schools and so forth. He didn't seem to believe that we hadn't any relations, we had to spell it out about a hundred times. And he took some time to understand that our parents really were incommunicado. And he didn't seem to grasp that Barb

91

and Sid were nothing to do with us whatsoever. Practically the first thing he did was to ask them if they couldn't be *in loco parentis*. Barb nearly burst a blood vessel, and I'm bound to say, so did I.

"Absolutely not!" she said. "I made that quite clear to Dr Warden. My husband and I are here purely and simply on account of my mother's decease." (Decease — I ask you!) "We shall stay until after the funeral, and then go straight back to Birmingham. We do have children of our own, you know."

"Oh, quite, Mrs Dark. I quite see that. It's simply that this is an unusual case, to say the least. These aren't at all the kind of children we'd expect to have to take into care. And yet it begins to look as if it might be the only alternative."

"You mean you'll have to send somebody to look after us?" I asked.

"This has to be classified as an emergency," Mr Parrish said. "Three children, all under age, left without legal guardianship. You're absolutely certain your parents said nothing about guardianship, or left any instructions in case of this kind of eventuality?"

"They said Mrs Bartle was our guardian," I told him. "They said we were to do as she told us, even if we didn't agree. How were they to know she was going to die? She wasn't all that old."

"Oh, quite," Mr Parrish said. "No one could have foreseen this — misfortune. But what about your parents' solicitor? Might they have left instructions with him, do you think?"

"Old Barrett?" William said. "I doubt it. They did see

him sometimes, I think, but Dad was always saying what an old woman he was. They thought he fussed too much."

"Barrett . . ." Mr Parrish made a note. "That will be of Barrett, Charles and Noon. I'll contact him first thing tomorrow. There's just a chance."

"Not much, I should think," I said. "After all, they *made* the best arrangements they could."

"Hmm. Well. But the position is this, I'm afraid. Unless Mr Barrett has instructions to the contrary as regards legal guardianship, you immediately become the responsibility of my department."

"It's very kind of you," William said. "And we appreciate it. But we shall manage perfectly OK by ourselves."

"I'm sure you would," Mr Parrish said. He looked really worried then. You could see that he was a nice bloke with a job he didn't particularly want to do. "But I'm afraid it's right out of the question. We have a legal responsibility, you see. It's entirely for your own protection."

Incredible as it now seems, even then we didn't fully understand. We didn't understand that people can be done good to absolutely against their own will. Especially if they are children — or minors, which is the legal word they use.

"But you've done that, now, Mr Parrish," William said. "You've been and checked that we're OK, and we are. And you've offered us your help, and we're very grateful. And obviously we'll give you a ring if we run into any trouble."

"Yes, thanks very much, Mr Parrish." I was keen to get him out of the house. I felt uneasy. Our own house was being taken over by strangers — first Barb and her ever-lasting Sidney, and now this man from the Council. I couldn't wait until we were left alone together, just the three of us.

But he didn't go. Heaven knows how long it took him to get through to us that he never would until he got us what he called "committed into care". It's a terrible expression, and sounds like going to prison, which is more or less exactly what it means. All three of us, against our will, were to be moved out of our own house, straight after the funeral, and put in foster homes — unless, that is, we could quickly find someone we knew to take us in.

To say that we were thunderstruck would be the understatement of the century. We were pulverized. Lucy started to cry. She already had a thing about step-mothers, on account of what she'd read somewhere, and you could see that she thought foster mothers were about the same thing, only worse. That's logical enough, when you think about it. At least with a stepmother you usually have your own real father around, even if he doesn't tend to be much help in *Snow White* and *Hansel and Gretel,* and so forth.

I put my oar in.

"Move *out*? Why? Why can't you put someone in here, if you've really got to? Why can't someone like Mrs Bartle come and live in?"

"It's not part of our system, you see." He sounded apologetic, I'll give him that. He could see our point of view, all right. "It's not Department policy. Fostering takes place in the home of the foster parents. But ideally, in a case like yours, which I'm bound to say is very uncommon, we'd try to find a family whom you already knew to become temporary foster parents."

"Mrs Chick would!" Lucy was really sobbing. "I want to go to Mrs Chick, or Mr Poynton. I won't go into an orphanage, I won't! Don't let them, Oliver!"

My own heart was hammering by now, I admit it. We were being made prisoners, and there was nothing I could do. Something told me that sure as hell there would be something in the regulations about children not being in care of old ladies who hobbled about on sticks, or old men on the Pension. (There was, too.)

"Our parents did try to leave us with one or two people they know," William told him. He had gone white. "But there's rather a lot of us. And we don't know all that many people all that well. But they might change their minds now all this has happened. I'll ask them."

He wasn't allowed to. He had to give Mr Parrish their names and addresses, and *he* would ask them.

"You see, they have to be made fully aware of the responsibilities involved," he said. "And undergo certain formalities."

That, I guessed, was that. If people were going to be vetted and inspected, and have to sign about a million forms in triplicate, nobody we knew was going to get involved. They'd be scared off. Letting someone come and stay for a while was one thing. Being made a foster parent by the Council was another. And I'm bound to say that none of the people our parents had originally

95

tried seemed *remotely* like foster parents, to me. In fact, the idea was so funny I nearly laughed. My friend Nigel's mother, for instance — Mrs Bradbury. Playing bridge five nights a week, and always got up as if she were off to Buckingham Palace to pick up her life peerage. She didn't look like *anybody's* mother, for heaven's sake, not even Nigel's.

We all sat there, in our own sitting room, while our whole world fell about our ears. It was like a nightmare. I kept thinking that any minute I would wake up and find it wasn't true. I shut out the sound of Mr Parrish's voice and tried to picture an ordinary Sunday afternoon, with Mum and Dad buried behind their papers, telling us to clear off for half an hour and give them some peace. And then we'd all go somewhere together. To the park, or a stately home, or a zoo, or just to walk by the river. Then I tried to picture the front door opening and then the door of the room, and them both being there. And how they'd laugh at what Mr Parrish was saying, and offer him a cup of tea, and then see him politely out. And then, when he'd gone, we'd all have a good laugh together. Because it was ludicrous, I could see that, and so would they, if they were here. But that's the whole point of a nightmare. It's ludicrous and horrific at the same time. And in our case — true.

When Mr Parrish had gone we were numb with shock. It is a terrible thing to have to admit, especially after what I've said about death being so enormous, but we were more stunned than we had been the day before. But perhaps I shouldn't feel guilty about this. Dad says that everything in nature has a built-in instinct for survival.

Barty's death hadn't threatened our survival, but this did. Not literally, of course, in the sense that anyone was trying to kill us. But we did feel threatened. I had never felt so scared and threatened in my whole life before.

We went up to Lucy's room to talk because we couldn't stand the sight of Barb's smirk. She was triumphant, I swear she was.

Lucy still obviously hadn't taken the situation in. William and I had, but we hadn't really accepted it. I suppose we were too used to tackling problems and making them turn out the way we wanted.

"Can I go and ask Mrs Chick if she'll have us? I know she will."

I doubted it. Lucy, perhaps — but not two boys the size of William and me, one of whom (mentioning no names) was among the gang who used to shout "Chick the Stick!" after her, before Lucy stopped us. And as I said before, it was perfectly obvious that the Council could never allow it. There's an age limit for people who adopt children, and Mrs Chick was light years above that. And fostering is a kind of adoption, so it was bound to apply.

On the other hand, it didn't seem a bad idea to get Lucy out of the house for a while. It would cheer her up to go and sort through Mrs Chick's cards.

"Go on then, Lucy," I told her. "Ask her."

She trotted off downstairs.

"Gordon Bennett!" I said. "What a mess!"

"You see now why Mum and Dad are always going on about bureaucracy and red tape," William said. "We're up to the neck in it ourselves, now."

He sounded considerably bitter.

"Where the hell do they think they're going to send us?" he said. "Not anywhere round here, that's for sure. *You* know anyone round here that does fostering?"

I didn't. I'd practically never heard of it till now.

"And what about school, if we end up the other side of town?"

I hadn't thought of this.

"They wouldn't, would they?"

"Course they would, fool! They'll send us to whoever'll have us. You don't think they care about us, do you? All they care about is getting us slotted in somewhere and off their hands, and getting a rubber stamp in the right places on their bloody forms."

William practically never swears — not at home, anyway. We do at school, of course. As a matter of fact, the form I'm in are the biggest swearers in the school. We're known for it.

There was a commotion going on downstairs. Old Barb screeching again and Lucy shrieking like a polecat (whatever that sounds like — but I've read it somewhere). She came stamping up the stairs and flew in. Her face was scarlet. Another tantrum.

"She won't let me!" she screamed. "I'm going, I am! I *can* go, I can!"

"Calm down, Luce," William said. "Of course you can. I'll tell her."

William isn't basically the one who sticks up for Lucy — I do it as a rule. But I think we both realized that as eldest he had a better chance of telling Barb what was what.

He did, too. He told her that Lucy had an open invitation to visit Mrs Chick and did so practically every day, with our parents' full approval. She had also gone with *Barty's* approval, he told her. You would have thought that would have settled it, but not on your life. Barb started going on about her and Sidney being in legal charge of us until we were "taken into care", as she put it, and about how she didn't know about other people, but *she* took her duties seriously. William told her that she wasn't our legal anything. Boy, he was really cool. He asked her if she'd signed any forms, and that floored her.

"There you are, then," he said. "We all appreciate your concern, but Lucy must be allowed to go."

William has this great knack of putting people down and being so polite about it that they can't do a thing. Barb then went off on a tack about Lucy being attacked on her way there or back. Hopeless bat.

"If you really think it possible that she will be raped in broad daylight between here and the next avenue, then Oliver and I will take her and bring her back."

I wish I could've seen Barb's face when William said "rape". I bet it really brought the red spots out. Worse than "dead" in her book, I should think. She didn't call a spade a spade, she called it "a digging implement" — as Dad would say. Anyway, she sure as hell shut up, and William called up and I got Lucy and we all walked out of the house together.

We left Lucy at Mrs Chick's and told her we'd fetch her in an hour. Then we went to the park and watched this football game that was going on.

The funny thing was, that once we'd been there for a time, the whole situation we were in seemed to have faded. It seemed absolutely unreal. I mean, it was just like any normal Sunday, with people standing around with their breath making smoke, and stamping their feet, and little kids running up the ladder to the slide, and people walking dogs. It was the same kind of feeling I'd had the day before, when we went out shopping after they'd taken Barty away. It made me realize why people sometimes go missing when things get too awful. It sounds mad, but it seemed to me that as long as we stopped out, so long as we didn't go back to the house, the whole horrible situation didn't exist.

8

It's lucky I keep a diary. It's more a journal, really, because I will write a lot some days, and hardly anything on others, in one of those page-a-day diaries I've been getting for Christmas for the last two years. I don't use them for appointments or anything, just for putting down what has happened, or how I feel about things. A lot of what happened in the next few months I wouldn't be able to tell in exact order if it weren't for my journal. Time went absolutely haywire, from the very minute Barty died.

Usually, funny as this may sound, I can *see* time, in a kind of curve, like one on a graph. And weeks I can usually feel as a rhythm, with different colours for each day of the week. I can't remember when I first noticed that each day was a different colour, but it was certainly years back — when I was about Lucy's age, I think. I've never actually discussed this with anyone, but I expect people have their own private time maps.

My time graphs and colours were shot to hell. Life seemed all disjointed and broken into unconnected fragments. This really threw me. I was like a traveller in the desert who has lost his compass. Because the future is always a blank, you might say that all life is like a desert, so it helps to have something like a time graph to hang on to.

The Monday before the funeral, for instance, didn't feel like a Monday at all. Come to think, it didn't feel like *any* day of the week. It was on its own — and so was the Tuesday.

For a start, we didn't go to school. It just happened to be half term, but we wouldn't have gone anyway. As William said, we weren't about to go out and leave Barb and Sid in sole possession of our house. And Janet was due in the afternoon, with her husband and sensitive kid.

Sensitive. I wish you could have seen him. Around twelve stone, at a guess, I'd say. He could have beaten old Barty on the draw to the biscuit tin, any day of the week. I'm not saying it's not possible to be sensitive *and* fat, I expect it is. But you can take my word that this Stephen was about as sensitive as a pickled gherkin. His mother called him "dear" or "pet" in every other remark. This really got me.

Janet's husband was called John — or Mr Gates to us. Lucy thought this was hilarious, because anything further from the Janet and John in the books she knew, you could hardly imagine. John was a draughtsman and didn't talk much. He didn't even talk much to Sid, which seemed peculiar. They seemed considerably embarrassed with one another — probably because all too often they'd heard one another being taken apart by their wives. The only conversation I heard them have that lasted more than two minutes was one about football. If you could call it a conversation.

102

The only good taste either Barb or Janet showed, so far as I was concerned, was that they hated one another's guts. They didn't show it, of course, not openly. But they sniped, non-stop. From what I could gather, the main trouble was that they were each terrified that the other had got more than her — more money, I mean, or worldly goods. Barb had got a new dralon suite, and Janet had the latest washing machine. Barb had been to Majorca last year, to a four star hotel with a swimming pool, and Janet was going this year to a five star one, with two pools. That sort of thing. It must have been really interesting to be around when that pair were trying to split Barty's worldly goods straight down the middle. It would have taken King Solomon to sort them out.

I said this to Lucy, after they had had a particularly frosty session about their carpets, and she said, "P'raps they'll saw everything in half. You can't saw babies in half, but you can tables. It'd be really funny. Half a chair, half a sideboard, half a bed — "

"Half a telly," I said. You could really see the funny side of it, put like that, though nobody could say it was funny at the time. From then on, whenever they were doing their sniping, Lucy would nudge me and whisper "Half a frying pan", or "Half a front door", and this, while the humour did wear off in the end, at least had the effect of putting things into perspective. And we did it so often that even to this day if anyone's carrying on like that (not that anybody else could, quite like that) one of us only has to say "Half a bottle opener" or "half a fish slice" and the rest of us know exactly what it means.

Everyone else is naturally mystified.

I am not going into a long description of the funeral. This is not because I think it would be morbid, but because there is no point in it. What happened to us after the funeral is more important.

In the end, William was the only one of us to actually go to the funeral. His motives for doing this were a bit mixed, I think. He said he was going out of respect, and to represent our family, and that Mum and Dad would have wished him to. This is what he said to Barb and Janet, who were against the whole idea, on the grounds of morbidity. His real reasons were partly to annoy them, and partly plain curiosity, because he had never been to a funeral before. In a way, I wouldn't have minded going, for the same reasons, but I wasn't about to leave Lucy back at home with sensitive Stephen.

On the morning of the funeral there was an incident I will relate about Stephen. It is not absolutely necessary, but does throw a light on human nature, and is also quite funny. At least, I think so. You have my permission to skip it if you like.

I've already told about Barb going on about how sensitive Stephen was, and of course Janet thought this even more — said so, at any rate. It was practically her favourite word. Could she have another blanket for the bed, dear Stephen was so sensitive to cold. What a good thing there were other children for Stephen to stay with while the adults were at the funeral — such a sensitive boy, you know.

Well, we were all sitting round having breakfast on the Tuesday, and the funeral was to be at 11.30 am. We were having the whole shooting match — cereals, bacon and eggs — plus two slices of fried bread for the Boa. (We called him this amongst ourselves because we reckoned he could swallow a rabbit whole, if pushed, and also because if he overheard us he would think it was Boer, and not have his sensitive feelings hurt.)

I am bound to say that the prospect of attending their mother's funeral had not affected the appetites of Barb and Janet. They tucked in like anything, and even had Radio 1 on in the background, which does not exactly go in for funeral marches. If anyone was doing any picking at their food, it was we three. Then, all of a sudden, right in the middle of a conversation about something different — probably the price of dralon suites — Stephen came out with, "I wonder how long it takes?"

He had his mouth full at the time.

"How long what takes, darling?"

"For the worms to get in."

This stopped everyone in their tracks. I knew what he meant, all right, and I should have thought everyone else would have done, but instead of telling him to shut up, and not talk with his mouth full, Janet said,

"For the worms to get in *where*, darling?"

Daft bag. He told her, all right.

"Into the *coffin*" he said. "How long it takes for the wood to rot, and then the worms and maggots to get in and start tunnelling into the corpse. I didn't even think worms *had* mouths, I thought."

"I think that will do, thank you." Barb's voice was stretched as tight as an elastic band, and the red spots were there again.

105

"Something must get in there and do some eating, else why would there be only bones when you dig them up?" He sounded really thoughtful, I'll give him that. As if he'd pondered for a long time.

"Did you hear me?" Barb was up into her parrot octave.

"I think, Barb, it would be better if you left things to me," Janet said.

"At breakfast! Worms! Ugh!" Barb shuddered. Worms affected her, even if death didn't.

"I only *wondered* . . ." Stephen evidently realized he'd put his foot in it, and was trying to creep round his mother.

"I don't know what all the fuss is about," Sid said. This was practically the first remark I'd heard him make off his own bat, and it must have been somewhat of an occasion, because they all turned and looked at him. He went red, the way ginger-haired people often do.

"Worms don't enter into it," he said. "It's to be a cremation."

That, I am sorry to say, did it. Everyone went into hysterics — by which I mean we three did. Looking back on it, I can't quite analyse why, except that I suppose none of us, to be honest, wanted to think about Barty being down in the earth with worms all over her, even though she wasn't our mother, and it was just plain relief. Anyway, we shoved back our chairs and fled. Obviously it looked bad to be in fits of giggles. We all went into Lucy's room and giggled ourselves sober.

William had to go and put his suit on then, ready to go. Barb and Janet, needless to say, were got up to kill — so to speak. They didn't wear black — one was in turquoise and the other in pink — but they did wear hats. My guess is that when they turned up the vicar must have thought he'd got his dates mixed, and was supposed to be doing a double wedding.

When they had gone the house went very quiet, and I began to think about Mr Parrish from the Children's Department. Up till then I suppose I had pushed him to the back of my mind, hoping he would go away. As it happened, I'd only been thinking about him for about five minutes when the front doorbell rang, and it was him. It wasn't enough of a coincidence to bear out the Theory of Synchronicity, but it shook me, just the same. Especially as William wasn't there. I asked him in, and my heart was really hammering, like it did once when I was about seven and I'd opened the door to a gypsy who pushed me on one side and walked straight in. A wild thought crossed my mind that he had come to take us away, and that when William got back, Lucy and I would be gone.

He asked where William was and I told him, and he said he was sorry he'd had to come now, but unfortunately it was imperative. That was the word he used — imperative.

Apparently he'd been on to old Barrett, but drawn a blank.

"Mr Barrett tells me that he did suggest a more structured form of guardianship, but your parents had thought it unnecessary."

"They thought he was a real old woman," I said. "Dad once said that if he followed every piece of advice old

Barrett gave him, he'd be bankrupted within a year, paying solicitors' fees."

Mr Parrish gave a faint smile and then started to tell me the arrangements he had made for us. He said he was sorry that to begin with we would have to be split up. He apologized for everything, all the while he was explaining. Lucy and I were to go to someone in West Byford, right the other side of town. Our worst fear came true. And William was to go to some other family.

"It's only about a mile from where you and your sister will be," he said. "You won't be completely out of touch."

"As near as makes no difference, we shall," I told him. "It's dark by half past four."

"And it will only be temporary, of course. I'm sorry, but it's the best I could do at such short notice."

"And then what? Can we come back here and someone look after us?"

"I told you. I'm sorry. There's nothing in the regulations to cover that."

My parents, I knew, would have blown up at this point — even swearing. "Bloody system!" they'd say. "Bloody regulations!" But I didn't. It was as if a cold wind was blowing round me — indoors, in our kitchen. I shivered. I wondered how to tell Lucy. I remembered a potted biography I'd read about the way Rudyard Kipling and his sister were left by their mother with a family at the seaside, and the way they were treated. God, it was awful.

"What if we don't like it?" I heard myself say. Ask a silly question.

"Well, of course, we all hope that you'll settle down quickly and life will go on more or less as usual."

You can always tell when grown-ups don't believe a word they're saying.

"Mrs Chivers has fostered short term for us before, and there've never been any complaints. And she has a son of around twelve, so that will be a bonus."

Twelve. Do people who are trained in child care really believe that someone who's nearly fourteen wants to sit watching Superman all day with a twelve-year-old? (As a matter of fact, this thought of mine was almost prophetic, except that he didn't just watch it, he thought he *was* it.)

"I don't feel like a foster child," I said. "It's nothing to do with me."

He didn't know what to say.

"God," I said. "Isn't life bloody awful?"

He smiled. For the first time he lost his apologetic look and truly lightened up.

"Come on," he said. "If you saw some of the things I see. Every day."

I asked him what sort of things, and he told me some, and it did make me feel better, as it was meant to. All those kids with broken-up families, and parents that beat them, and living out their whole lives in care, some of them. There was no need for us to feel sorry for ourselves. At least we had something to look forward to. We knew that it would end. And it wasn't even for a year, or half a year. Just a few months. And we had each other.

"I'd better have a word with Lucy now," he said.

"I think I'd better explain. She'll take it better from me. You've got to know the way her mind works."

He smiled again.

"OK. You'll be all right?"

He asked me to put William in the picture as well. He was very busy, he said. He left the two names, and addresses of where we were going, and asked for us to be ready, packed, by half past four. One suitcase each.

When I'd let him out I went up to tell Lucy and begin packing. Lucy and Stephen were in her room playing Monopoly. Funny, the way all through those awful days we kept going back to Monopoly. Because it's got a framework, I suppose, and life hasn't. Life spills and spreads all over the place. Monopoly never changes — all those well-known names — Old Kent Road, Islington, Pall Mall, Vine Street — right round the board. Even Chance and Community Chest are always the same, and they can never truly break anyone, like real-life chances can. It's a lovely safe ritual, Monopoly. Lucy the boot, William the car, and me the iron. And nine times out of ten I'd get the Coventry Street block early on, and end up winning.

I looked at the board. He was playing with my iron. And he was cheating, I could see that at a glance. Nobody gets that amount of money *and* property early on. He was exactly the sort that would cheat against a seven-year-old, and under different circumstances, I'd have pitched into him. As it was, I said,

"Better pack it in now. I've got something to tell Lucy."

"It won't take long," he said. "I've nearly won."

"I can see that. But it might take longer than you think, now I'm here."

That at least let him know that I knew.

"I don't mind stopping," Lucy said.

"That's because you're losing."

"No it's not, then! It's because I'm sick of Monopoly! We're always playing Monopoly!"

So she'd noticed, as well. She was nearly crying, and didn't really know why. It sure as hell wasn't because she was losing. At that moment I'd have given anything, absolutely anything, for Mum and Dad to walk in through the front door. Instead of which I had to tell Lucy about Mrs Chivers, and help her pack.

When I told her, she did cry. I sat on the bed with my arm round her. I looked round her room, with all its little scattered farms and battles, and her whole world was wrapped up in there, I knew it. And I cursed to hell the people who were doing this to us. I wondered whether if I wrote to the Queen it would do any good.

When Barb and Co returned they looked chirpier than they had when they left. William, on the other hand, looked upset. Old Barty, after all, had looked after us the best she could, and the only real harm she'd done us was in dying.

Old Barb dished out some of Dad's sherry all round, though whether it was supposed to be for their nerves, or as a celebration, was anybody's guess. She was certainly already stuck into the question of the will, and arranging to meet Janet at Barty's cottage to divide things up.

"Half a lampshade!" I said out of the corner of my

111

mouth to William, who to my surprise let out quite a squark. This, he later said, was due to the sherry. He hated the stuff, and only had it (two glasses) because he thought it would miff Barb and Janet, which it certainly did. When Barb said she thought he was rather young for sherry, he replied that if he was old enough to attend a funeral, he was old enough to have a sherry afterwards, and that he'd been having it since he was twelve. This, of course, was an outright lie, but I did not blame him for it.

You won't believe this, but not one of them said one word of sympathy to us. They just downed their sherry, packed up their things (and Barty's) and then stood round clucking and wondering whether the car to fetch us would be on time. When Mrs Fowles came round and heard what was going to happen she sympathized, and started saying, "Oh, you poor things," and so on, and this irritated the hell out of Barb and Janet, you could see that.

"I'm sure this kind of thing happens every day of the week," Barb said. "It's not the end of the world."

Which inane remark shows exactly what kind of a daft bat she was. People get run over every day of the week, for heaven's sake, and are killed, and it *is* the end of the world, for somebody. However common awful events are, it doesn't make them less awful.

Leaving the house was much worse with them being there. We couldn't say goodbye to it properly. It was like coming back from a holiday without one last look at the sea. Unfinished business.

It all seems a blur from when Mr Parrish arrived and people started turning off electricity at the mains and

112

cancelling the milk and emptying the bread bin for the birds. I did manage to stand and have a last good look at my room, which I'd always taken for granted until then. I just stood and looked slowly round, and I didn't exactly say a prayer, but I did almost.

Then we all left more or less together. Barb was obviously trying to make a good impression on Mr Parrish, and as we left called after us the barmiest thing she'd said to date:

"Goodbye, children! Be sure to write!"

I ask you! Write. To her. Words fail.

9

The first part of the drive was through familiar places — past the park and the City Crematorium, and then right through town and over the river and into unknown territory. It was probably trees and grass being missing that made it seem strange. There were factories and warehouses, and mixed in with them rows of tall thin houses. Lucy sat huddled in the back seat with me, staring at it, and I wished the view was better, for her sake.

Mr Parrish tried to keep up some cheerful conversation. I tried, as well, to begin with, to put him more at his ease, because he was still apologizing. It wasn't his fault, I knew that. And if people apologize too much it gets on your nerves.

It was dusk, and lights were going on. The road we turned into when Mr Parrish said, "Well, here we are!" had those orange sodium lights. It was a side road, but quite wide. The houses were all semi-detached, with those square bay windows with net curtains. They all had low walls in front, with not exactly a garden, because you couldn't have had a lawn, but a few steps to the front door, and a few flower tubs.

"Well, then, Lucy and Oliver!"

Mr Parrish got out and we followed.

"You're about a mile further down, William. On the left, opposite the swimming baths."

William's face had a funny pinched look. I expect mine had as well. Personally, I was trying hard not to cry, and had been for most of the day. But at least I had Lucy. He had nobody.

"We'll come straight and see you," I said, and he nodded.

"I'll just go and have a quick word with Mrs Chivers, if you don't mind waiting here for a moment." Mr Parrish was apologizing again.

We were glad of a few minutes on our own.

"We're *miles* away from home!" Lucy was shivering. Her teeth were actually chattering.

"Only a couple of bus rides," I said.

"We'll meet every day," William said. "Try to."

"Right, we will!" Though I didn't see how.

"Are they on the 'phone, do you think?"

We looked up. There were no wires.

"Never mind. *You* might be and then we can ring from a call box."

"I've just remembered!" Lucy wailed. "My money snail! I've forgotten it!"

Lucy's Money Snail was one of the barmiest objects you have ever seen. It was a family joke. She'd won it at a fair by rolling ping pong balls or something, and when Dad first saw it, he said that it would have been luckier to have lost. It was a truly repulsive object, in green and yellow tin, and you posted the money through a slot in its shell . . . But Lucy liked it, and in any case it was full of her money.

"I've got some money," I said. "I'll lend you some. We can always go back and get it in a day or two."

"We'll have had *burglars* by then!" she wailed.

I had to laugh, and so did William. Old Lucy's sense of the dramatic coming out.

"It's not funny!"

"I tell you what. If it is burgled, I'll get you another. I'll go round every fairground in England till I win you another."

"You never *would*! Nobody ever wins on those ping pong balls, you said so yourself. You said so when *I* went on them. And then when I won, you said it must have been a miracle, and you were going to write to the Pope. You did! I remember, if you don't!"

"Buy you another, then," I said.

Mr Parrish came back.

"Here we are, Mrs Chivers. This is Oliver, and this is Lucy. Their older brother, William — who of course will not be staying with you."

We looked at Mrs Chivers. She wasn't all that different from Barty, only younger-looking. Her hair was frizzy, and her eyes were quite small.

"How do you do, Mrs Chivers," I said. "It's very kind of you to have us."

"Hello," Lucy said.

"Oh, it'll be a pleasure," Mrs Chivers said. "I'm sure we shall all get on as right as rain. If you can just bring their things in, Mr Parrish. Their tea's nearly ready."

She turned and went back into the house. We began to move our things from the car under that weird sodium

116

light. We didn't talk. William must have felt worst of all. He helped carry the things.

"In the hall," Mrs Chivers called from somewhere at the back of the house. "Just put them down, and my hubby'll take 'em up when he gets back."

The passageway was lit by a bare light bulb, but was quite dim, even so. The floor was covered with green patterned lino, and the walls were painted brown half-way up, and then cream.

"What do you think?" William asked out of the side of his mouth on our next trip to the car.

"Dunno," I said. "All right, I suppose."

That's what I said. It wasn't what I thought. I thought it looked horrible, just as bad as I'd imagined. And Mrs Chivers hadn't exactly given off vibrations of motherly warmth. She'd hardly even looked at us. Lucy came running back to us.

"I don't like it!" she whispered. "I don't like it!"

It was a fierce, desperate kind of whisper.

"Don't worry, Albertine," I whispered back. "It's just that it's different, that's all. It'll be OK. And we're together, remember."

Mr Parrish joined us, still looking apologetic.

"All set?"

"Yes."

"Oh William! Goodbye, William!" Lucy wrapped her arms round him. He lifted her and she kissed his face and he kissed her back.

"See you soon, menace," he said.

He put her down and she started to cry.

"Well — goodbye for now," I said.

"Yes. I'll see you soon."

William and I just stood there. It's funny, really. We didn't know what to do — hug, shake hands — what? We'd never had a real parting in all our lives, so we just stood there. It was like getting on to a stage, and then your mind going a complete blank because you hadn't had a rehearsal.

"You'll see each other at school tomorrow," Mr Parrish said. "Hop in then, William."

Lucy and I stood and waved when the car drove off. William's face was just a blur. At that moment I felt that I was the eldest, and not him. He was setting off on his own, and I wanted to protect him. Lucy was crying quietly. She wasn't putting on one of her big shows. There was no point. There was nobody to hear her, and nothing anybody could do.

"Come on, Albertine." I put my arm round her shoulders and we turned back to the house. The net curtain in the front window moved, and I caught a glimpse of a face.

When we reached the front door I almost knocked before going in. I felt like an intruder, going into the hall. A boy came out of a door on the right. He was wearing a Superman T-shirt. My heart plummeted.

"You the new ones?" He was chewing gum.

I nodded.

"Shut the door, will you!" Mrs Chivers shouted. "There's no point my lighting fires for them to go straight out the front door."

I shut the door. We followed the boy through the door at the end of the passage. There was another bare light

118

bulb, and a smell of ironing. Mrs Chivers was in there, sawing bread like planks.

"Shut that door, as well," she said. She didn't look up, but then she had to mind her fingers.

"Fetch us the sardines, will you?" she said.

The boy went down two steps at the other side of the room and came back with a tin of sardines already opened. I could smell them from where I was. I nearly threw up. God, I thought, just our luck. Our first meal, and it has to be sardines. At our house, we don't just not like them, we loathe them. Everybody has some food that makes them feel sick even to think about. It's tapioca pudding for some, or spinach, or bacon fat. With us, it's sardines. I watched Mrs Chivers dig a knife into the tin and then squash the silvery mess on to a slab of bread and marge, and wondered how long I could hold the sick down.

"Where's the loo, please?" Lucy's voice came out as a squeak.

"The what? Oh, the toilet. Up the stairs, first on the left."

Lucy shot out. I heard her feet clattering up the stairs and hoped she would be there in time. She gets actually sick, Lucy. She doesn't just feel it, she *is* it. I thought of her up there on her own, heaving into the lavatory bowl. Usually when she's sick Mum's there with her, and holds her head, and tells her she's all right. I'm afraid I am too much of a coward for this. The minute I see, or smell, somebody else's sick, I throw up. At school I always get sent out of the room the minute anybody starts, because people are fed up with having to clear up two lots of

119

mess. Mum says this is because I have a highly developed sympathetic nervous system. That's not what everybody else says.

I watched the oozing grey and yellow being scooped from the tin and spread.

"Look, Mrs Chivers," I began.

"What?" She said it mechanically, still spreading.

"I really am terribly sorry, I honestly am. You couldn't possibly have known, but the thing is, Lucy and I don't like sardines."

"Rubbish," she said. "You're not going to be faddy, I hope? You weren't expecting salmon, I suppose?"

"It's just sardines. Everyone in our family hates them. It's sort of inherited."

"Well, we have 'em here regular. They're good for you. Heard this man say so on the telly."

"But they make us sick!" I said desperately. Lucy would be back any minute.

"All the more for us, then," she said. "Plain bread and marge be all right for you, will it?"

"Oh yes! Thanks!" I couldn't have been more grateful if she'd offered us turkey with all the trimmings.

"Turn the telly up, will you?" she said to the boy.

We had gone from the frying pan into the fire, so far as television was concerned. Mrs Chivers left old Barty standing. She had it on all day. Sometimes the sound was turned down, but she kept flicking her eyes towards it in case she was missing something. Sometimes she'd have the radio on at the same time, and then the effect was really weird. There would be someone rabbiting on about how to make raisin cakes on the radio, and a

120

picture of an earthquake or something on the TV. Schizophrenic.

When the sound on the set had been turned up she sat down and started to pour tea."

"Here you are, then." She pushed a chipped cup over the oilcloth. "Don't take sugar, do you, I hope?"

"Neither of us do, thank you," I said. "Mum and Dad say it's a . . . "

My voice trailed off. She was ladling two heaped spoonfuls into her own tea and stirring it noisily. Funny, old Barty used to do that. Some people can almost make a career out of stirring things.

I had been about to tell her what Mum always said about sugar, especially the white variety, and it was not good news. At our house, it was practically on the Poison List. It was lucky I stopped in time.

"It's a terrible price, sugar," she said. She said it to herself, not to us. "Go and fill this pot up, will you, Cliff?"

He had taken his tea and a couple of sandwiches and was sitting with his back turned to the table. I could see the bulge in his cheek.

"I'm watching this."

"You do it, then," she said to me. "Through there."

She jerked her head, but didn't look at me. The whole time we were there she hardly once looked at either me or Lucy.

I took the teapot and went down the couple of steps into a tiny scullery. There was an even stronger smell of ironing and old vegetables, and a depressed-looking budgie hunched on its perch in a cage. Lucy wasn't

121

going to like that. She gets very fervent about birds and animals in cages, and once, when she went to a zoo on a school outing, refused to go any further after about the third cage. The teacher who had to sit with her in the coach while the others went round was very enchanted, as you can imagine. And when Lucy was around four, and I was nine, Mum took us to a circus. Lucy cried so much we had to come out after half an hour. *I* was pretty fed up about that, at the time, though now I'm older I suppose I can see her point of view.

I filled the teapot and went back up the steps. At the same minute Lucy reappeared in the doorway opposite.

Her face gave me a real shock. It was white. Dead white, except for smudges like bruises under her eyes. It probably sounds ridiculous, but I was terrified. There was nobody to look after her but me. I knew that was true. I knew it already. Mrs Chivers was *responsible* for her, all right, but only in the sense of giving her a roof over her head and enough food. She didn't *care*, in the real sense of the word. Lucy, with all her funny panics and dramas, and moods like quicksilver, was going to be a mystery to this Mrs Chivers, I knew that. And a mystery she wouldn't even try to solve.

I felt sick to my stomach, and more frightened than I had ever been in my whole life before. More frightened than when I had found Barty. Everything that had happened to us in the last few days had seemed to threaten. First there was poor old Barty. Then we'd been invaded by her awful daughters. And now we had been cast loose in the world at random, it seemed. It all tasted like a nightmare, or one of those Grimm's tales that you always find yourself half believing in. No wicked step-mother, no grinning witch, could ever have been more cold and strange than that woman sawing bread. I don't really remember how we got from then to bedtime. I only know it was horrible. I know that I was so afraid, and felt so alone, that I started my real journal that night.

All that I have written so far I've done from just quite short entries in my journal, and from memory. But from that onwards I wrote practically every single day. I did it partly because I wanted *evidence* — If that's the right word. Something told me that in the weeks or months ahead we were often going to be unhappy and frightened. Even badly treated. I didn't, of course, think we were going to end up in the oven, or given poisoned apples. But I read newspapers, and watch television, and I did know that horrible things could happen to children — sorry, minors — even in this day and age.

But the second reason I took to writing this day-by-day account was more a personal one. I hope that at this point you are not going to laugh. I began to write my journal as if I were writing — or speaking, really — to a friend. There was no one I could tell things to, so I told them to my journal. And where I probably got the idea from — and this is where I am sticking my neck right out and risking that you *will* laugh — was from the Diary of Anne Frank.

All right. So I'm the first to admit that there is no comparison between being taken into care and going into hiding from the Nazis. That was life and death. I know it. I cried over that book, I may as well tell you. Especially over things like where she tells the kind of gifts they gave on birthdays, like one fresh egg, or a made-up poem or a bar of chocolate. But there *is* a comparison. Anne Frank and I were both lonely, and needed to speak our inmost thoughts. When I say "lonely", I don't mean literally alone. She was with her parents, and her elder sister and a boy around her own age. And I had Lucy and William. But Anne Frank couldn't share what she was really feeling with any of her family, and nor could I. Lucy and I are on the same wavelength, all right, but for heaven's sake she was only seven, and I had to keep up a good front and make her think I was strong and someone she could rely on. And as for William, we get on all right, but basically we're *not* on the same wavelength. William doesn't talk a lot about feelings. This is why I was so staggered when he told me that he was in love. You could have knocked me down with a feather.

In any case, it wouldn't have been fair to tell my true feelings to either Lucy or William. I had to keep up a brave face, just the same as they did. *They* must have wanted someone to confide in just as much as I did. But they were brave, and hid it as much as they could. In our family, we call this "tin soldier", after the fairy tale. And I'm sure it's right. You can't go round in life spilling your feelings all over everywhere. If everyone did that, life would be absolute hell.

But it does nobody else any harm and can do yourself a lot of good if you can let off steam by writing down how you feel to yourself — or rather, not *exactly* yourself, but the way Anne Frank did, to an imaginary friend. She called hers "Kitty". It's a nice name, I think, safe

124

and warm-sounding. No one called Kitty could ever condemn you, or turn you away. It's a name that snuggles close, and Anne Frank told her Kitty every single thing, even down to details like embarrassment about using the lavatory, or having to use waste bins instead, and the way she was spiteful, or hurt her mother's feelings. I doubt whether there is a real Kitty in anybody's life. There's never *anybody* you can tell everything to. This is true whether things are going well or badly. We all have secrets that we will never tell to anybody. Never tell to anybody *real* I mean. The truth is, you have to make your own Kitty.

And this is what I did. I did it without really knowing why at the time. And that night, in a strange bed in a cold strange room, I waited until I knew for sure that Lucy was asleep, and then took my journal from my suitcase and began to write. And for the first time I didn't write it in the ordinary way. I wrote the date, and then, I expect, I sucked my pen for a minute, and then began:

3rd November

Dear Mr Jung,
I am writing this to you because you are someone I think I will be able to tell my inmost thoughts to, and also because you were the first name that came into my head. I know this fact will appeal to you, because you believe in free association. I also agree with you on the subject of coincidences, and in fact had my own theory about this

before I even read your book.

It is now 9.30 pm and I am sitting up in bed writing. It is very cold. Lucy is already asleep in the top bunk. That doesn't mean to say she won't wake up screaming with a nightmare, in fact I think this more than likely. She is subject to nightmares, and the events of the past few days have been enough to give them to anybody. You will certainly understand this. I know what importance you attach to dreams, and so do I, up to a point.

Today has been a nightmare in itself, and even as I write now I feel unreal, as if I were in the middle of a bad dream. I can see our cases still unpacked on the brown and green lino. In a way, I'm glad they are still unpacked, because at least that is a sign that we are only here temporarily. On the other hand, it makes you feel homeless, and that is not a good feeling.

I hate it here. I may as well admit it. I hate her, I hate him, and I hate their awful son. I'll tell you about them. She is about forty-five or fifty, I think, though I'm not much good at guessing ages, especially women, who can trick you with make-up etc. (Not that she wears any.) Anyway, it doesn't matter how old she is. To look at she is short and dumpy, her hair greyish and scraggy and her feet in slippers edged with fur. This means she doesn't walk, but shuffles. She might shuffle in her outdoor shoes, for all I know. She sure as hell shuffles in slippers. She is penny-pinching, bad-tempered and rude. It was pretty rude of her to say she wondered what kind of parents went polling off to South America and left their children unattended. Then, when Lucy went pink (which was quite a relief, really) and blurted out, "They

126

didn't! And they didn't know Barty was going to die!' she just sniffed and said, "I suppose you're encouraged to answer back your elders and betters at home. But I want none of it here, thank you, madam."

That's a phrase I really hate — "elders and betters". It's idiotic. As if the older people get, the better they are automatically. Not in my experience. If they're bad to start with, it's ten to one they'll get worse. Hitler didn't exactly end up as a saint, nor Idi Amin, and nor will Mrs Chivers either.

Mr Chivers' name is Fred and he's a storekeeper. He is also creepy. At the moment I can't say why I feel like this about him. He seems to be under Mrs Chivers' thumb (whose first name, by the way, is Joan) and he calls her "My dear" quite a lot, and also "mother". He's pale and thin and his hair is getting thin too, and his eyes seem to flicker from the corners in a sly way. Not all the time, but quite often, and especially when he looks at us. He seems as if he's hiding something, and as if underneath his meek look there's quite a different person hiding. His face is just a mask.

As for Cliff, words fail. He's gingery, with a pale face and freckles, and his hands are freckled too. He may be freckled all over, for all I know. He has shifty, wishy-washy eyes. From what I can gather he has two main interests in life. One is watching TV, and the other needling whoever happens to be fostered here at the time.

But it's only temporary, and Lucy and I are together. I certainly hope William has got somewhere better than this. He's on his own. Perhaps there might be a beautiful

127

girl there and he could fall in love with her — if, of course, I'm not underestimating the strength of his feelings for Carol. I don't think so — not from what I've read or heard.

I'm cold now, in fact shivering. Thank you for listening.

Goodnight.

Yours sincerely,
OLIVER SAXON

4th November

Dear Mr Jung,

I have plenty more news to tell today. I'm writing this up in our room again. It's only just gone seven, but Lucy was so whacked she could hardly keep her eyes open, and she's asleep already. I suppose I could write this downstairs and pretend it was some homework, but anything is preferable to sitting with those three and some crummy TV quiz game, and in any case, you never know, Lucy might wake up. I've put my dressing gown over my clothes because I hope to go down later and scrounge a snack as I'm still hungry.

We went to school today. Mr Parrish did say he thought perhaps it would be better if we took the day off to allow us to "adjust" as he put it, to our new surroundings. But Mrs Chivers said she didn't want us under her feet all day, and as far as we were concerned the feeling was mutual. The day we ever adjust to this set-up will be the day it rains coke.

The school isn't too bad. For one thing it's right next to

Lucy's. The minute we set off we felt better — just to be out of the house, I suppose. It sounds ridiculous, but I had a real rush of happiness and excitement to my head, as if we were setting off on holiday. The world outside seemed so fresh and normal, and it put things into perspective. A comparison would be with a prisoner coming out of his cell and back into the world, though I admit this is putting it rather strongly.

Even old Lucy started skipping, so she must have felt the same. At breakfast she'd looked so white and goggle-eyed I hoped she wasn't going to be sick again. It doesn't exactly endear you to a new school if you're sick the minute you get in there. We talked about how horrible breakfast had been — just plain sliced bread with marge and jam, though Mrs C did say she'd got some cornflakes for tomorrow.

You'd have thought she would have taken Lucy to her new school on the first morning — having said which, we were both glad she didn't.

"What if people thought she was my *mother*" Lucy said. "Ugh!"

"Daft old bat," I said. "*And* fat. Looks like the mother of a Cliff. Get it? Cliff — cliff . . ."

We both fell about laughing, feeble as it was. If you laugh at people they don't have any power over you.

The schools were both called Lockwood — Lockwood Junior and L. Comprehensive. This rings a bell with me — something to do with *Jane Eyre* I think. It could've been the name of that awful charity school she went to — I'll have to look it up. Anyway, there's no resemblance, I'm happy to say. Lucy's Head was really

129

nice, and her class teacher is very young and pretty and called Miss Bowles. In some ways I think Lucy would have been better with someone older, more of a mother figure, but there again, when you're Lucy's age everyone over about eighteen looks old enough to be your grand-mother, let alone your mother. She was happy enough when I left her, and when I picked her up said she'd had a great time and had made a clay model of a Tyranno-saurus Rex. This was good news. She's nuts about any-thing prehistoric and has got about a million books on the subject. You might say it's her collective unconscious or subconscious, or whatever. You know what I mean.

Now for my school. Not all that different from my other one — home from home. Just that there were only two familiar faces, and one of those I could have done without. I didn't meet William till break, and even then we didn't have time to say much, because Cliff spotted us and then hung round staring and listening. When William and I finally got together alone in the lunch break, he said he could certainly see what I meant about Cliff. The family he's with are called Bates, and there's just the mother and the son called Trevor, who's left school and is an apprentice plumber. We compared breakfasts, and he certainly scored on that, having had sausages and beans on toast. The only snag was he'd had to get up practically half-way through the night to eat it, because of Trevor having to catch an early 'bus. A case of the early bird getting the worm.

He seemed to think his place was all right, though, knowing William, he would have said so anyway. He's much more philosophical than I am. Sometimes when

130

I'm getting aereated about something, he'll just shrug and say, "Time passes. All things pass." Every now and then I punch him when he says this.

I'm in a class of around thirty, and most of the work seems the same as at my old school. Still, at the end of the day I was considerably shattered. William and I haven't made any plans to meet out of school yet. Lucy was very chuffed when he came along with me to pick her up. You'd have thought she hadn't seen him for a hundred years.

We had scrambled eggs and bread for tea. Mrs Chivers doesn't seem to have heard of toast. Query: Shall I introduce her to this startling innovation?

The only interest she showed in our new schools was to say "Got on all right, did you?" while still buttering — or rather marging — bread, and not even looking at us. Lucy and I muttered something like "Yes, thank you," but if we'd said well, actually the caretaker knifed us, and we were mugged in the lunch break, I doubt whether she'd have turned a hair. The matter was closed. To be perfectly fair, she doesn't show much more interest in her own son.

While we were having our tea, she said, "Weren't expecting butter, I hope?"

I said, "Oh, no. We nearly always use margarine at home. My mother says it's much healthier."

Mrs Chivers said "Oh!" as if this was news to her. I had the feeling she was disappointed. She *wanted* us to like salmon and sugar and butter, so that she could have the pleasure of telling us we couldn't have them.

I think I was more homesick for Mum and Dad then

131

than I'd been the whole time they've been away. At home, when we got home from school there was nearly always something really nice to eat, like sausage and mash, or corned beef pie or cauliflower cheese. And we'd have it in the kitchen while Mum asked us about school and Dad teased Lucy. They know the names of nearly all our teachers and friends. But I have to keep reminding myself that we're very lucky to have parents like that, and just to be without them for a few months isn't the end of the world.

Mr Chivers seems to get home just before six, so he had tea separately, I'm glad to say. He slurps his tea and also clicks his dentures. This may be a fault or it may be an affliction, but either way it's pretty repulsive. He said to Lucy, "You're a pretty little girl, aren't you?" and the look she shot him would've turned him to stone if it had been in mythology.

Cliff said, "I saw their brother today," just as if Lucy and I weren't there.

"Oh, yes?" said Mrs Chivers. "What's he like, then?"

"Lanky," said the toad. "Long hair and glasses."

"Long hair?" she said. "Got growing it the minute his ma turned her back, I suppose. While the cat's away the mice will play."

"As a matter of fact it's been long for some time, Mrs Chivers," I said — politely, I hope. "My parents have no objections."

She did look at me then, for once. More stared than looked.

"Don't they indeed!" she said. "I'll tell you this. No son of mine'd go round with horrible greasy hair

132

hanging to his shoulders."

"It's *not* greasy!" Lucy'll always stick up for people. "It doesn't have to be greasy to be long!"

This struck me as plain logic, but not so Mrs C.

"Nobody asked your opinion!" she snapped. "I don't need a seven-year-old teaching me my business, thank you very much! And *your* hair's getting long enough to be getting out of hand. Take the scissors to that, I daresay, some time when I've a mind."

"But I'm *growing* it!" Lucy went stiff from top to toe, the way she does before she goes into a tantrum. "It's a scientific experiment and I'm growing it for pigtails. Mummy measured it before she went away, right down to the last millimetre! And she's going to measure it again, the day she gets back!"

Mrs Chivers looked absolutely pie-eyed at all this. She was knocked sideways, you could see that. She didn't even reply. In the end she just sniffed and got up and went into the scullery. From there, after a minute, she shouted through, "*If* she ever gets back, you mean!", which is about the lousiest remark I have ever heard any adult make to a seven-year-old. I kicked Lucy under the table and rolled my eyes, and to my relief she rolled hers too.

After tea I offered to wash up. This was not out of kindness, but an attempt to keep Lucy from seeing that tatty little budgie for as long as possible. She offered to help and my heart sank, but luckily Mrs Chivers said "It don't take two to rattle a few pots about. You get next door to number 63 and ask Mrs Foster if she's finished with her books. She'll know what you mean."

133

Before stopping, I must tell you what the "books" turned out to be, because it really throws a light on human nature and will interest you. They were a sort of cross between magazines and paperbacks, and were true Romances with pictures of people kissing on the cover, and titles like *When Love was Lost* and *The Stricken Heart* and other such bilge. Old Lucy had a quick look at them before bringing them in, and told me when we came up for her to go to bed. She giggled while she was telling me, and that set me off too. The thought of Mrs Chivers, fur-edged slippers and all, sitting there lapping up True Romances was absolutely ludicrous.

"P'raps *she* was in love," Lucy said. "With *Mr* Chivers! Oh lummee!"

Writing it now, it doesn't seem funny so much as sad. Nobody could compare Mr Chivers to a knight on a white charger. The fact that Mrs C needs romances shows that she *believes* in true love, even though this seems impossible. When she got married, I expect she did believe she'd live happily ever after. And now look at them!

Anyway, I expect you'll be able to analyse this. I'm really glad I chose you to write to, because you're interested in this kind of thing, and won't be bored by it.

I'm so tired now I don't feel hungry any more. So I'll just say goodnight and go to bed.

Yours sincerely,
OLIVER SAXON

November 5th
Guy Fawkes

Dear Mr Jung,
Just a short note in case you think I've forgotten. Have only just got back from a bonfire, and will tell you about it tomorrow.

Yours sincerely,
OLIVER SAXON

November 6th

Dear Mr Jung,
I am certainly lucky to be writing this with my own two eyes, considering the shambles last night. We went to a street bonfire about half a mile away, and the toad naturally went too. Normally, Lucy stays in on bonfire night. This is not because she is a coward. She is as brave as a lion, but simply doesn't like loud bangs. As a matter of fact, I may as well admit I'm not crazy about them myself. But I'm very keen on the jacket potatoes and hot dogs aspect of things — and even more so this year, for obvious reasons.

The good thing was that William came along as well, because the bonfire was about half-way between our two places.

Hell fire, it was one of the worst things that's ever happened to me. It was black as pitch because it was on some waste ground away from any street lights. This meant there was only light from the bonfire — and that wasn't much. And people (including that bloody toad) could keep lurking about in the background. Which they certainly did. I thought all bonfires were supposed to be

135

supervised, but if this one was, I sure as hell didn't notice it. There were maniacs creeping about all over the place setting off fireworks — and even quite tame ones, like Green Smoke and Snow Fire, are no joke when they suddenly fizz up about a foot behind you. Lucy was yelping and screaming, and in the end shaking like a leaf.

William said, "Let's get out of here before we're blinded or something."

So that's what we did. I'd spotted a chip shop on our way there, so we went and got some and walked slowly back eating them.

It was almost like old times, just the three of us walking along together eating chips out of a bag. I can't remember what we talked about, but when we were about half-way (and we weren't hurrying, I can tell you) an ambulance went by, with its blue light flashing, in the opposite direction.

"They'll be going to pick up the dead and injured from that bloody bonfire," William said.

I turned and watched, and it *did* turn left along the road we'd taken earlier. When we reached Manvers Road we stopped on the corner.

"No need to go back yet," I said. "They think we're at the bonfire. Or perhaps you'd like to come in, and I'll introduce you to Mrs Chivers, and she'll give you a nice cup of tea and hot toast with lashings of butter."

Lucy giggled.

"I thought of a name for her today," she said. "The Shred."

"Shred? Why?" I asked.

"Marmalade, silly. Chivers Golden Shred."

"As a matter of fact, it isn't," I told her. "It's Robinson's Golden Shred, and Chivers Thick Cut. Come to think, that fits Thick Cut."

"Well, I'm going to call her the Shred," she said. Her being obstinate was probably a good sign of her being more her own self again. Anyway, nicknames are another good way of cutting people down to size.

"OK," I said. "The Shred it is.'

With the weekend coming up we started to talk about what chance we had of getting back home for a few hours.

"We could look for my Money Snail," Lucy said.

We discussed whether or not to say where we were going, whether to pretend we were doing something else. William seemed to think his Mrs Bates would let him go, but I wasn't so sure about Mrs Chivers. "On the other hand," I said, "if I say I'm taking Lucy swimming, for instance, it's ten to one the toad would say *he* wanted to go."

We were still discussing this when the police car passed us. It wasn't sounding its siren or flashing its light, but for some reason I had a flash of terror. It was a premonition, all right. It drew in and stopped bang outside number sixty five.

"Gordon Bennett!" I said. "That ambulance we saw! It must've . . ."

"Oooh . . . He must be dead!" Lucy's voice went up in a thin wail.

"Don't be silly." I put an arm round her, and hoped she couldn't feel my heart thudding.

"Think we'd better go back now?" I asked.

"Want me to come with you?" William said.

I remembered Mrs Chivers' remarks about long hair. If there had been any trouble at the bonfire, Mrs Chivers would immediately suspect William of being the ringleader on account of his hair.

"Better not. Look — what about tomorrow?"

As we made our arrangements the door of the house opened. The policeman came out, followed by Mrs Chivers, still tying on a headscarf. We watched them both get into the car. I stared at the tail lights of the car till they dwindled into nothing, as if hypnotised.

"What if . . ." Lucy's voice was very small. "What if he's dead?"

"Not him!" I said, though I didn't know — how could I? "More likely burnt the seat of his pants!"

Lucy didn't giggle as I'd meant her to. Lucy generally giggles at any word like bottom, belly button, bosom, lavatory and so on down the scale. Dad says she's in a scatalogical stage.

"Burnt his bottom," I added. A little high-pitched squeak that was nearly a giggle.

"We'd better get back," I said. I didn't relish the prospect.

"I'll come round first thing in the morning," William promised. "Find out what's happened. Cheer up, Lucy. Not the end of the world."

"It's not *you* that has to live there! Oh, I don't want to go back! I want Mummy and Daddy!"

"Come on, Albertine." I began walking back towards the house. Her shoulders were shaking beneath my arm.

138

"See you tomorrow, William."

Mr Chivers was sitting smoking in front of the television. I hadn't seen him smoke before. Perhaps his wife wouldn't let him. While the cat's away the mice will play, I thought.

He looked at us for quite a long time with his watery eyes. Then he turned back to the screen.

"We saw the police car," I said.

"Did you, now?" He looked at us again. "And what else did you see?"

"Well, not all that much," I began. "Because we didn't really stay — "

"We saw an ambulance! With its blue light flashing. Was it Cliff? Was it?"

"Saw an ambulance, did you? Ah, yes, that would've been for him, all right."

"Was he hurt badly?" I asked. "I'm terribly sorry."

"Sorry?" His voice turned sharp from its usual whine. "Why should you be sorry?"

"Well — anyone would be. Of course we are."

"Ah." He paused. "Not sorry we've *done* something, then?"

"*Done* something?" Then the penny dropped. "Oh no — no! We weren't even there! We only stayed about half an hour."

"Prove it, can you?" he said. "Got an alibi?"

"We were with William," Lucy said. "And we didn't do anything, of course we didn't! I don't even *like* fireworks. I wouldn't even have gone if we'd been at home."

Mr Chivers looked at her thoughtfully.

"Now then, little girl," he said, "don't take on. There's

139

no harm going to come to *you*."

I didn't much like the way he emphasized the last word.

"I want to go to bed," Lucy said. "I'm tired."

"Ah, now," he said in this horrible soft voice. "I don't think that'll do. Oh no. Mrs Chivers'll want a word, you see. She said so. Make sure the little devils — you'll pardon the expression, but them were her very words — make sure them little devils is here when I get back. I shall want a word, she said."

"How long will she be?" I asked. "It's long past Lucy's bedtime. I could wait up for her on my own."

"I want to stay with *you*," Lucy whispered. She clung to me, and he gave us another of his long, beastly looks.

"You come and sit on my knee, if you want a little rest," he said. He actually patted his knee. "Come on, my pretty," he said coaxingly, "you're not afraid of your uncle, are you?"

Lucy *really* clutched on to me then. Gordon Bennett, was he mad? Sit on his knee!

"Come on," he said again.

"She doesn't actually like it, Mr Chivers," I said. "Sitting on people's knees. In fact, she hates it."

This of course was a downright lie. As I've said before, Lucy has a very affectionate nature, and is always putting her arms round people and hugging them, and so forth.

"We'll just sit here and wait," I said rapidly, pulling Lucy down next to me on the sofa. "Please don't bother about us. Just carry on watching as if we weren't here."

"Oh, I couldn't do that," he said. "Wouldn't be

140

manners, would it?"

A slow smile went over the lower part of his face, leaving out his eyes. It was then that I knew why my first instinct had been of dislike, why I had thought him "creepy". He was tormenting us — slowly, softly and relentlessly. He was getting pleasure from his power over us.

Terror washed over me. I had known adults who bullied or were spiteful or nagging, adults who shouted and even hit people. But this was different.

"Funny . . ." he said. "You don't *look* wrong 'uns. Especially the little girl."

He looked again at Lucy.

"We aren't, Mr Chivers," My words didn't come out as loud and firm as I'd meant them to. "I told you. We weren't even there."

"Ah," he said. "And *why* wasn't you there? Meant to be, weren't you? Got leave to go to a bonfire — should've *been* at the bonfire. Simple as that, sonny boy."

"If you really want to know," I said — and this time my voice *was* loud, "it's because it was a shambles. No one was in charge, and people were chucking fireworks all over the place. It was dangerous. If we hadn't left, *we* could've ended up in hospital."

"Ah." He seemed almost to be purring. "And asked Cliff to go along with you, did you? Took *him* out of harm's way?"

"Well, no. As a matter of fact . . ." My voice trailed off. I couldn't quite bring myself to tell him that Cliff was one of the ones doing the chucking.

141

"I wonder why?" he said. "You the oldest, and meant to be in charge?"

I stared at him. They were going to make out it was my fault.

"Look," I croaked, "I really ought to get Lucy to bed. It's hours past her bedtime."

For a long time, it seemed like an hour, he just looked at us, first at one, then the other.

"I'll tell you what," he said. "Why don't you go and put the kettle on? Then the little girl can have a nice hot drink and go to bed."

I didn't suspect a trap. I got up and went down into the little scullery. I had picked up the kettle and started to fill it when Lucy came flying down. She practically fell down the steps.

"Oliver, Oliver! I want to stay with you!"

As I turned, the scullery door slammed shut. There was the sound of a bolt being shot. I put the kettle down and stared over Lucy's head at the closed door.

We were in there till nearly eleven o'clock. I didn't call out, or even try the door. I was more afraid of Mr Chivers than of being held prisoner. Lucy and I spoke in whispers. We played the Professor's Cat for a while, but in the end Lucy fell asleep, curled up on a mat. I shall always remember how it felt to be in there, with the awful smell of wet clothes and fusty vegetables. The tap dripped non-stop, like a clock. The moth-eaten budgie pecked listlessly at its seed. Before she fell asleep, Lucy said she meant to set it free on the day we left. I personally did not feel this was a good idea, but kept quiet. Once or twice the budgie did seem to say some-

142

thing. It sounded like "Poor little bugger", but perhaps this was me projecting what *I* felt. More likely it was saying "Sing to mother," or some equally futile remark that bird-owners go in for. We know some people with a cockatoo that says, "Hello, chubby-chops!" to everyone who comes into the room. The owners then fall about laughing, and say how clever. You'd have thought the novelty would have worn off. I have yet to hear a bird say anything sensible.

I shall spare you a blow-by-blow account of what happened when Mrs Chivers finally got home. Suffice it to say that it was a nightmare. Lucy woke up and began to cry when Mrs Chivers banged the scullery door open. I asked how Cliff was but never got a proper answer. She was ranting on about being "half-blinded" and "marked for life" and was blaming me for the whole thing. I was the oldest, and was responsible for him, she said — regardless of the fact that he would have gone anyway, even if we hadn't been there. It was no use arguing. I just stood there, and every now and again said, "Sorry", to which she shrieked, "I'll give you sorry! I'll give you sorry!" and so on and so forth.

I was sorry, of course. But not in the sense of apologizing, because my conscience is quite clear on this score. But sorry he'd been hurt. However loathsome someone is, you don't want that kind of thing to happen to them. In the end she ran out of steam, and told us to go to bed — which was what we'd been wanting to do for the last three hours. She hit me on the side of the head as I went past. It didn't really hurt, but was a terrible feeling, all the same, because it showed how much she hates me. It is not a good feeling when someone hates you.

You may be wondering how I have managed to write so much today. This is because it is now nearly one o'clock on Saturday, and Lucy and I are still in our room. Mrs Chivers says we are to stay here all day. She has gone to the hospital, but he's still down there somewhere.

The worst part of this is that we can't go home as planned. Lucy kept a look-out for William as I've been writing this, and he came just after ten. We talked through the window, keeping our voices down, of course. I told him what had happened. We are not actually locked in, because the door doesn't have a lock, but William advised me not to just walk out the house. Lucy started to wail about her Money Snail.

"I'll go to the house on my own," William said. "I'll find it and bring it round. Either tonight, or in the morning,"

Apparently his Mrs Bates has gone to visit her sister for the day.

I watched William walk away, and envied him because he was free. Now that Lucy and I couldn't come, he'd probably ring Carol and ask her round. Lucy is trying to make a game of being shut in, and says it's like Rapunzel. Like hell it is. I expect it's her way of coping with things, though. You'll know more about that aspect of things than I do.

Gordon Bennett! The door just opened, and there was Mr Chivers. I nearly hit the roof. He must have literally crept up, because the linoleum on the stairs makes them really noisy. He probably thought he'd catch us out doing something, though I can't think what. If so, he was disappointed. There was me sitting on the bed writing this, and Lucy lying on the floor doing a jigsaw.

His excuse for coming up was to say he'd opened a tin of soup and put it on, and that he'd bring mine up to me, but Lucy could come down and have hers with him. Needless to say, she turned down this generous offer flat. He mumbled something about running up and down stairs waiting on us, so I offered to come down and carry the soup up myself. He just shut the door and went away, leaving us not knowing whether we'd get anything to eat or not.

"Bed knobs and bottle openers!" Lucy said. "What a pig, what a villain, what a double-dyed rogue!"

Her speech is quite picturesque for someone of that age. She obviously liked the sound of the words, because she kept muttering them under her breath as she slotted in the pieces.

There's not much more to tell at the moment. I think I'll lie back and shut my eyes and think of all the things to look forward to when Mum and Dad get back. Food is figuring quite a lot at the moment. Probably the same syndrome as thirsty people in the desert seeing mirages of water. I can conjure up the sight and smell of, say: bacon and eggs (the bacon done really crisp), steak and kidney pie, roast lamb with roast potatoes, peas and beans and mint sauce, chocolate mousse, treacle sponge and custard.

What visions, what bliss! And what a reflection on human nature that all I can think of is my stomach. On the other hand, this is quite natural. Dad says that only when man has satisfied his basic instincts is he free to pursue other interests and activities i.e. you can't practise your guitar on an empty stomach.

Hey ho! Here comes the soup.

OLIVER SAXON

November 7th Sunday

Dear Mr Jung,

The second day of the incarceration of the younger Saxons — or Rapunzel Chapter Two. I think I'm a very bad subject for this kind of situation. If everyone had, say, a week locked up in a room, they'd all be able to appreciate the Diary of Anne Frank a lot better. You think that you can imagine how she felt, *I* thought I could imagine. But you can't. You have to actually experience a thing to know what it is like.

Anyway, I'll fill you in on events to date. The first thing is — Cliff's home. Mrs Chivers and he came back in an ambulance yesterday afternoon. Lucy and I watched from behind the curtain. One eye is covered and both his hands are bandaged. Here's another interesting slant on human nature for you. Despite her having gone on about it all being my fault, etc etc, she'd no sooner got into the house than she set about Cliff. This is about the only good thing you can say about the Shred. She's as foul to her own son as she is to us.

You can't have any sympathy for him, even now. You won't believe this (or perhaps you will, with your knowledge of human nature) but Cliff has told them that we deliberately ran off and left him alone at the bonfire. He has also accused us of chucking fireworks, and

146

denied that he did himself. We hadn't even *got* any fireworks, for heaven's sake. But we could say this to the Chivers till we're blue in the face, and they wouldn't believe us. Mrs Chivers called us liars. Lucy started to cry. Anybody who knew us would know we wouldn't chuck fireworks, let alone lie about it afterwards. But I have a helpless feeling. Nothing will make that pair believe us. I even offered to swear on the Bible. She then said things were bad enough without dragging the Bible into it. She probably hasn't even got one.

She says she's going to ring "the office" tomorrow. She's welcome. If they move us from here it can't be to anywhere worse. It might turn out to be lucky for us, Cliff having that accident.

William came this morning. He'd found Lucy's Snail and is going to bring it to school tomorrow. He said, "Cheer up! The house is still there, the same as ever." It's all right him talking about cheering up. As far as he's concerned, things are going quite well. Anyone can be optimistic about other people's troubles.

It's a bit sad to think that it's Sunday, and at home we'd have had roast beef or lamb, with roast potatoes and so forth. Here, we've only had bread and marge, some soup, and a banana each. And it's freezing cold. On the other hand, to look on the brighter side, I'm actually looking forward to going to school tomorrow. Usually Mondays are not in favour with me.

Had better stop now. Lucy wants a game of Monopoly. So do I. Its properties and houses feel more real to me than this one.

It's a real pity you can't write back and give me some

147

advice. It would be even better if I could talk to you. You might be interested to know that for an essay we had to choose anyone through the ages we would like to meet, and describe a conversation with them. I chose you, and I got B plus! Most people only got Cs and Ds, because they chose such crummy subjects. Half the boys chose Olivia Newton John. I ask you!

I will keep you posted on further news.

Best wishes

OLIVER SAXON

November 8th Monday

Dear Mr Jung,

Not a lot to report today. Cliff didn't go to school, so that was a bonus. On the other hand, Mrs Chivers was in a really foul mood on account of this. When we got back from school she told us she's been and rung "the office" and left a message for Mr Parrish.

"I've told him I want you gone by the end of the week," she said.

It was a great temptation to say "Likewise".

I expect she told them all kinds of lies about us, so let's hope they don't swallow them. The trouble is, that when an adult says one thing and a child another, people tend to believe the adult. This is illogical. Like what I was telling you earlier about "elders and betters". I wonder what Ma Chivers was like as a kid. The mind boggles. You can hardly believe she ever was.

I've got two lots of homework to do now, so will sign off.

OLIVER SAXON

November 9th Tues

Dear Mr Jung,

Again, not a lot to report. Cliff has to go to hospital again tomorrow. I'm bound to say for someone who's supposed to be "half-blinded", he's pulling in plenty of telly viewing. Apparently Mr Parrish hasn't been in touch yet, so she says she'll ring the office again tomorrow. She says, "They'll put you in a home where you belong." She means Home with a capital H, of course. In other words, no kind of home at all.

Funnily enough, they announced on the TV that later on there's a programme about Children in Care.

"We'll watch that," says Mrs C.

"Oh Mum!" groans Cliff. "I wanted to watch Superman!" — or a western, or whatever muck.

"*You'd* better watch it, as well," says she to me and Lucy.

It might be a good idea. If it's any good, I'll tell you about it tomorrow.

OLIVER SAXON

Nov 10th Wed

Dear Mr Jung,

The news is that Mr Parrish called round here today while we were at school, and on Saturday we are to be moved to a Home called Highlands. It can't be all that far away, because we're still to go to the same school. God knows what lies old Chivers has told him about Lucy and me. Naturally, she's cock-a-hoop. I happen to know that she must be paid for having us, and I'm bound to say that with the food she's given us she must have made a

149

good old profit — Oliver Twist isn't in it.

We watched that programme I told you about last night. It was amazing. That bloody woman sat there saying things like "Poor little devils!" and "People ought to be ashamed of themselves, treating innocent children like that!" To hear her carry on, you'd have thought she was St Francis of Assisi or somebody. And it never occurred to her that Lucy and I were there watching too, and *knew* what she said was phoney. I felt like jumping up and yelling.

But I suppose she's quite good at putting on an act of liking children, or she wouldn't be allowed to foster. She must have pulled the wool over Mr Parrish's eyes. That's why I'm a bit worried about what she may have told him about us. You may think I'm making too much of this, but as a matter of fact this is one of my obsessions — or phobias. No doubt you know the correct term. It started when I read something in a newspaper about a man who had been wrongly convicted of a crime. He had been in prison for ages, but was to be pardoned and let out. Query: How can you be pardoned for something you didn't do? Anyway, our whole family was discussing this, and I said that if *I* were imprisoned for something I hadn't done, I would yell and yell and yell absolutely non-stop until they realized I really meant it. I couldn't imagine that this man went all those months in prison as meekly as a lamb, when he *knew* he hadn't done it. None of the others seemed to think that all the yelling in the world would get you out. And that was when I had this nightmare thought that in life there really were stone walls that you could batter and batter and batter against, and it would be utterly hopeless. I feel frightened just writing about it like this. Surely there *is* such a thing as justice? Surely the truth wins over lies?

Well, I suppose I feel better to have got this off my chest and I hope you will find it interesting. You must have dealt a lot with complexes and phobias in your time. I think I might even go in for psychology myself. It must be fascinating to dig out the secrets of people's inmost hearts.

OLIVER SAXON

Nov 11th Thurs

Dear Mr Jung,

I might as well kick off with the worst. Last night Lucy wet her bed. I can't tell you how awful it was. When she woke up and realized what had happened, she just cried and cried. She was inconsolable. I kept telling her it didn't matter, and that it happened to everyone, and there was a boy in my old class that still wet his bed about twice a week. But it's different to wet your bed at home, when your own parents will be there and understand, and another for it to happen in someone else's bed. Particularly people like the Chivers.

Lucy begged me not to tell. She said we always made our beds before going to school, and no one would know. But the mattress was *soaking*. And the room is very cold, and she might get pneumonia, she *couldn't* sleep on it. And it would start to smell. God, it was awful.

That bloody Chivers was as foul about it as you might expect. She carried on about our parents paying for a

151

new mattress when they got back, and called us "spoiled brats". To hear her, you'd get the impression that both Lucy and I wet our beds whenever we felt like it, just for kicks.

Anyway, the whole thing made me sick. And poor old Lucy had to set off for school as white as a ghost except for the blotchy red round her eyes. I didn't know what to do to help her. Sod Chivers. Sod them all.

I'm going to put the light out now and get into bed. It's only half past eight, but I've got a feeling Lucy won't go to sleep till I do.

OLIVER SAXON

PS It is now half past ten, and Lucy can't get to sleep. I've tried telling her stories and all that, but she won't. She's as obstinate as hell when she wants to be. And she's got it into her nut that she won't go to sleep so that she can't wet her bed again. (She's on a camp bed now, by the way.) The poor little devil is lying there at this minute, watching me with her great staring owl's eyes in her white face. I'll pack this in, and try reading to her again.

Nov 12th Friday

Dear Mr Jung,

The good news is that this is our last day here, and the bad news is that William won't be with us at Highlands, at least not to begin with. Apparently he has to wait for a vacancy. Query: Do you have to book well in advance if you want to go into care?

Old Albertine finally got to sleep last night, by the way, about twenty minutes later. She's now whacked, needless to say, but quite chirpy, putting her things back in the suitcase. She keeps saying things like "I'll bet there's a colour telly", and "I wonder what the other children will be like?" as if she were going on holiday. I hope for her sake it'll be all right. There's no reason why it shouldn't be. After all, the people who run Homes do it as a full-time career, so they must like children. Also, the other kids there will be in the same boat as Lucy and me.

I forgot to tell you. The Shred knows a woman called Mrs Marchmont, or something, who goes in there to help out. She says the kids there are "proper little delinquents" and that bed-wetting is the order of the day, more or less. I think I by now know Mrs C well enough to take *that* with a sack of salt. Mr Chivers said at teatime, "Pity the little girl couldn't have stopped", with his usual leer.

Pity he couldn't have learned Lucy's name by now, as well. Lucy stuck her tongue out while he wasn't looking. She's now muttering to herself at the moment something about that frowsty budgie. She reckons the reason it's so dozy is that it's being poisoned by the smell in there. It is pretty foul, I admit, but I doubt if the fumes of wet washing and old vegetables could actually kill anybody. I pointed this out to Albertine, also the fact that if she let it out it would probably die of cold and starvation, or be killed by a cat. She saw my point.

All of a sudden *I* feel as if I'm going on holiday. I feel really excited and happy. We're escaping from here sooner than I dared hope. Good old Guy Fawkes. Good old Cliff. I'll write tomorrow and tell you about the next place.   Love,
                                        OLIVER
153

PHASE TWO

Dear Mr Jung,   November 13th Sat

Well, here we are at our new place, and you'll notice I've started a fresh page in its honour. You will also note the heading.

There's no doubt at all that this place is going to be better. Admittedly, we haven't met everybody yet, because they've nearly all gone to an away football match and will be back later. But that at least shows they're human.

Highlands is a big old house and there are ten children here. Mr Parrish has told us a bit about it. It's run by a couple called Mr and Mrs Warner, but when I say "run" I only mean they are sort of foster parents. In other words, we all help with washing up and running errands and so forth — just as if we were at home. It's run more as a large family than a hostel.

The only way you would know it's not an ordinary house is that the stairs are not carpeted. This is not meant as a criticism, just stating a fact. And of course this makes it seem more like a school. But all the actual rooms have carpets, and also it is centrally-heated, which is a nice change. Lucy and I have got rooms next to each other. They're really one room with a partition wall between, which is quite handy, because we can tap on the wall to each other. (This more from Lucy's point of view than mine. At her age you can get nervous at night,

154

even at home, let alone in strange places.)

We got here just before lunch, which turned out to be fish and chips from the very shop we'd stopped at on Guy Fawkes. (Slight coincidence, that's all.) Mr Parrish fetched them in his car, and he had some as well. He's really quite nice. I don't think Mrs Chivers has poisoned his mind against us. He was polite to her when he picked us up, and thanked her and so forth, but that was all. Whereas he was really nice to us, and never said a word about Cliff's accident or the bed wetting or anything. He teased Lucy about her Money Snail (which she was clutching in her hot little hands — didn't mean to leave it twice).

He has gone now, and Lucy and I are doing our unpacking. At least we *feel* like unpacking, which we never did at the other place. So that in itself is a good sign. Downstairs there's somebody called Mrs Tree, who apparently sometimes comes in at weekends and helps out. She seems quite nice and told Lucy what pretty hair she's got. She also asked her what she'd like for tea. I can't imagine the choice was *that* wide, but Lucy said sausage and scrambled egg, and that apparently is what we're getting. Better and better!

I'm thinking that now we've moved there's only really you who knows about our time at the Chivers'. I now have to make a fresh start, so that makes you really an old friend. I have been thinking that "Mr Jung" sounds a bit stiff, but obviously I can't call you Carl, so I wondered about a kind of nickname? These days, people often call psychologists "shrinks". I think this is quite a good name, and friendly-sounding, and from my point of

155

view makes you sound not so far away as "Mr Jung". Writing to you is really helping me, as I knew it would (thanks to Anne Frank!) So from now on, I would like to call you "Shrink". I hope this is OK with you.

This evening we'll no doubt be very busy meeting all the other members of the "family", and Mr and Mrs Warner, so I'll write tomorrow to tell you how we get on.

OLIVER

PS Usually I am superstitious about the 13th, but have decided not to be on this occasion.

Nov 14th Sun

Dear Shrink,

It's good to call you this for the first time. You really do seem to be an old friend by now. Yesterday was quite bewildering in a way, so it's good to have a time alone with you before embarking on today. (It's now 7am.)

By and large my first impressions of this place were right, and it is certainly better than being at the Chivers'. Everyone got back at around seven yesterday. They seemed very chuffed because their team had won. Some of them were leaping up and down the stairs three at a time and making whooping noises and chanting. They hardly seemed to notice Lucy and me. You can't blame them for this. Why should they?

Yet even as I write this I must be honest (because the whole point of writing to you is to tell the truth, and not just what sounds good) and say that I felt left out of things. All right, so they were excited. But they themselves must have been new here once. Didn't they remember how they felt? Mr and Mrs Warner seem nice — much younger than the Chiverses, and very jolly. If that's the word. It sounds old-fashioned but it fits them.)

We all had supper of baked beans on toast round a big table and that was when we met everybody. I can't remember them all at the moment, but will mention the ones I can.

1. Tracy. A girl of about fifteen I think, with a very pasty face and eyes that keep looking at you while you aren't looking, and then flick away. She's been here for about a year.

2. Billy. A boy of around ten. After supper he asked us why we were here. We told him, and he said, "My mum died as well, and I saw her dead. There was a fire at our house and she was all in flames. Bet you've never seen anyone burning up."

I wished he hadn't said this, because Lucy looked really sick, and it makes a bad impression at places when you're sick on the first day. Gordon Bennett, though, fancy seeing your mother die like that!

3. Mark, who is the oldest here and is seventeen. He is very tall and shooting his wrists and legs out of his clothes. Very quiet but seems nice, and smiled once, one of the best smiles I've seen for a long time.

After supper Mr and Mrs Warner asked Lucy and me to help clear up and wash the things. They said we could get to know each other better while we were doing it. But we'd only just started when the 'phone rang and she went to answer it and she called to him (his name's John) to come, and neither of them came back. Lucy and I didn't mind doing the dishes on our own. And obviously the Warners have their own lives and families outside this place. Must stop now — breakfast.

Later.

It's now seven o'clock and I'm writing to you before doing my homework. I've just read through what I wrote earlier and it seems as if I was a bit sorry for myself. Not really.

Anyway, today has been fine. For one thing we had a proper Sunday dinner with roast pork, roast potatoes, stuffing and so on. Then ice cream. Best meal in a long time.

Old Albertine has palled up with Billy and they've been playing in her room. I sure as hell hope he doesn't keep going on about his mother being burnt up. It's not him that'll have to get up if Lucy wakes up screaming with a nightmare.

I can't exactly say I've got in with anyone yet. In a funny kind of way, they don't seem the type for making friends. I don't know quite how to put it. They're not exactly standoffish. But they tend to watch you and wait and see what *you* do. I think the word is wary. But they all seem to like Kate and John (the Warners' names) and so do I. Particularly her. She's nearer Mum's age than old Barty or the Shred, and that makes her seem closer. (Not that old Chivers could be a mother substitute by any standards!) If anything, I'd say she was younger than Mum, and quite pretty, with long dark hair. I helped peel the spuds and then we had coffee and biscuits. She was asking about what had happened, and I told her about Barty, but didn't say much about Chivers, except

158

that we hadn't got on too well with her. About Chivers, she just said something about "any port in a storm", and laughed, and I did too. I feel just about back to normal now, and Lucy seems full of beans. You'll be glad to hear this, what with her wetting her bed. Not a sign, I good know.

I just broke off because Mark came in. My guitar was lying on the bed (not played since we left, but I expect I'll be able to here). He picked it up and strummed but he doesn't know how to play. I offered to teach him. We talked about pop music and so forth, and the groups we like. He then said I could come and listen to the end of the Top Twenty in his room if I wanted. I wasn't all that keen, but I went. His room is plastered with pictures and posters, mainly of girls. We had the radio on but he didn't really listen and was asking about the family, and where we come from, and so on.

There was one peculiar thing. When I told about Mum and Dad going off on their expedition, he said, "Well, that's a new one on me. Never heard that story before."

And it turned out that he didn't believe it, that he thought they had deserted us! And the more I said that they hadn't, the more he said, "That's what they all say", and "Nobody ends up in a place like this unless they've been dumped." I absolutely couldn't get through to him. To change the subject I asked him about his family, and he said he hadn't got one. He said he'd been found as a baby wrapped up in newspaper in a 'phone box. Query: Can this be true, and if not, why does he say it? I'll try to find out, and let you know.

It's now time to put the light out. Lucy's already

asleep. I just looked in, and it seemed so queer to see her lying in that bare room. Very different from at home, where you have to pick your way through an obstacle course of railways, battles and what all else. Given time, she'll put that right!

Goodnight, Shrink!

OLIVER

Nov 15th Monday

Dear Shrink,

Back at school. Most peculiar. A couple of weeks back, this was new. Now, going back there was almost like going home. Never thought I'd live to say that about school. Though as it's you I'm talking to, I may as well admit that I actually like it better than I admit, if you see what I mean! It's not exactly the done thing to say you like school. Same with the dinners. You're supposed to pretend they're pure poison. While we were with Chivers they seemed more like Lord Mayor's Banquets.

Saw Cliff at school and had great pleasure in giving him a good thump. (Neither blind nor maimed, I might add.) Let him go home and tell his dear ma about that. I would have done this anyway, without an excuse, but he gave me one by saying, "What's it like in the poorhouse, then?"

Speaking personally, if I had those two for parents, I'd rather live in a poorhouse/tent/chicken hut/rabbit hutch — you name it. What I'd really like would be for him to come round to our house when Mum and Dad get back — not invited, of course — catch me! — but accidentally. Collecting for something, perhaps, or a

160

sponsored walk. Then I'd open the front door and our whole family would be laughing in the background, and I'd see his jaw drop wide open — gunk! Then he'd see who lives in a poorhouse, and he might also get a faint idea of what a real family is like.

Sorry to go on like this. The truth is that since we had to leave home I don't feel so sure of myself. I mean, I actually catch myself wondering who I really am. It just shows how much we prop ourselves up in everyday life by having somewhere safe to go to, somewhere we belong. Even at school I sometimes feel I'm acting a part now — being "a minor in care", instead of me, Oliver Edward Saxon. It's weird — hard to explain. This is why perhaps I'm not making friends too quickly, and also why I spend every single minute I possibly can with William. I don't think he feels quite as uprooted as I do, and sometimes I get the feeling he wishes I'd go away and leave him alone. This must be because he's older. I don't think adults so much need propping up like this, more children. And I expect the younger you are, the less you are sure who you are.

And this makes me think that Lucy is probably the worst hit by all this. Last night I could hear her crying quietly through the partition. I didn't go in, because I think she'd have come to me if she'd wanted me. Poor kid.

It's a terrible thing to say, but just lately I've begun to feel really mad at Mum and Dad. I'm even beginning to think old Chivers was about right when she said what she did about parents who go polling off to South America and leave their children unprotected. Didn't it

161

occur to them that something like this might happen? They can't have thought very hard about it, if not. They knew very well that it wasn't even an ordinary trip abroad. When Kit Weaver's sister had meningitis their parents were in New York, but they picked up the 'phone and got them back in less than a day. They knew bloody *well* there aren't any 'phones in the jungle, and not even post offices, for that matter. I hope they feel really guilty when they get back and find out what's happened. They damn well deserve to.

I don't feel like writing any more. Sorry.

OLIVER

Nov 16th Tues

Dear Shrink,

Just a short note. The Warners took anyone who wanted to go to a movie after school. It was naturally some juvenile muck for the sake of the younger ones, and I didn't really want to go, but did because of Lucy. It was about the worst movie you could ever hope to see in a million years. Query: Where do people get the money to pay casts of thousands (including monsters) for a movie like that?

Goodnight.

OLIVER

Nov 17th Wed

Dear Shrink,

Spent most of the evening talking to Mark in his room. Although he's older than me (older than William, for that matter) we get along really well. He told me a lot about

162

his job. He's an apprentice plumber, and says that one day he's going to have his own business. He says he's going to have a house with a swimming pool, and at least two Rolls Royces. This all sounds a bit much, but when you think that he's been in care since he was born (in a telephone kiosk, don't forget) and doesn't even know who his mother is, you can quite understand that he dreams of something like that. In any case, it might happen. I hope for his sake it does.

You should have heard some of the stories he told me of various foster homes etc he's been in. It would make even your hair curl. Oliver Twist was born with a silver spoon in his mouth, compared with him. There was one woman he stayed with who gave him banana sandwiches for every single meal and saved up the money she was paid by the Council for a holiday, and then went off with her own sons to the seaside, and he was shoved back into a Home. And then there was another who used to lock him in his room every weekend because she said she couldn't trust him out of sight (shades of the Shred!).

It's a wonder he's so nice, after all he's been through. He must have a really strong character. He seems really interested in us — the family and so forth, and asked a lot of questions. He seems to have changed from that first talk when he didn't believe Mum and Dad would come back. Funny, that, because he was so definite about it. Perhaps he's been talking to the Warners and they persuaded him that my story *was* the truth. When Mum and Dad get back I shall ask him to stay.

Anyway, you'll be glad to hear I've got a friend at last. And Lucy gets on fine with Billy, who is only eight, it

163

turns out. He's got such long legs I thought he was older, but I suppose when you talk to him you can see he isn't. He's in there now with her and she's reading him *The Wind in the Willows*. I just sneaked a look, and there he is all curled up with his skinny knees under his chin, and sucking his thumb. So that makes two of them. Mum and Dad are trying to get Lucy to stop it, but she's taken it up again, I'm afraid. Understandable, as you'll agree, but I hope to God she doesn't end up with teeth like Debbie Palmer's. Talk about vampires!

Cheers, Shrink!

OLIVER

Nov 18th Thurs

Dear Shrink,

Not all that much to tell. Played table tennis with Kate this evening. She's really good. She put her hair in bunches to keep it out of her eyes, and only looked about sixteen! Afterwards we had coffee together and talked about all kinds of things. She's really easy to talk to — just like you, Shrink!

Mark put his head round the door a couple of times and beckoned to me, but I couldn't break off just like that. What it is to be in demand!

I mentioned to her the possibility of having a visit back home at the weekend, and she said that would be fine by her.

Nice for you to hear good news for a change!

Cheers!

OLIVER

Dear Shrink,

I'm only really writing today to keep my nose to the grindstone. No offence. What I mean is, that I know from bitter past experience that if you once start missing even one day in a Journal, the next thing is — wham! It's had it. I've got millions of journals with the last entry about February 1st!

Anyway, you don't drop old friends just because you've made some new ones, and by now I think of you as an old friend.

Cheers!
OLIVER

Nov 20th Sat

Dear Shrink,

We all went back to the house today, and I thought you might be interested to hear my reactions.

On the way there, on the bus, I think we all had the feeling of freedom. We're all OK at the places we're staying, but it was great to get away. And when we were on the second bus, from the town centre, on the route I know like the back of my hand, it was so terrific to see all the familiar streets and other landmarks that, ridiculous as it may sound, I felt a big hard lump in my throat. (It didn't get any further than that. I don't cry on buses, thank you very much.)

We *tore* from the bus stop and were gasping by the time we reached the back door. William opened it, and here was the first funny thing. I was suddenly scared to

165

go in! Don't ask me why. The nearest I can describe it, is that it was like Christmas morning when I still believed in Father Christmas. When we'd opened the stockings on our beds, we'd go downstairs to the sitting room to find our pillow cases. And I *could sense* that his presence had been there (which is amazing, because it hadn't!). I used to hang back and wait to let William go in first. And even then for the first few minutes the whole room — the tables, chairs, pictures on the wall, clock — seemed absolutely strange and foreign. I must have felt that they had witnessed something in the night.

This probably isn't a very good explanation, but it's the nearest I can get to how I felt today — not just for the first few moments after I'd stepped inside, but until we'd been round from room to room. It was a dull, misty day, and we went to put on the lights, clean forgetting that the electricity had been switched off at the mains. William then whispered (Query: Why did he whisper? Why did we all whisper?) that we wouldn't put any lights on, so as not to attract attention. I agreed. Query: Why did I agree, when it was our house, for heaven's sake? It must have been because for a time we felt like intruders — if not exactly breakers-in. We more or less whispered and went on tiptoe for the first ten minutes or so. We opened all the doors and looked inside. Lord knows what we expected to see. The air felt very damp and cold and our breaths were smoking.

When we got upstairs we only went into our own three bedrooms. Nobody mentioned this. But what it means was that we didn't want to go into Mum's and Dad's room, or Barty's — I suppose for obvious reasons.

Anyway, once we'd reached our bedrooms we loosened up. There was everything, just as we'd left it. Lucy swooped on to her Lego layout and was in there like a shot, sorting out the farmyards and Crusaders.

William went to put a record on, and remembered about the electricity.

"We'll turn it on," he said. "And the water. We'll want something to drink."

"And then to go to the loo," said Lucy, and giggled in her usual way.

So we switched them both on, and we decided it didn't matter if we switched on lights, and all of a sudden we felt at home again — really at home.

Time really flew by. We went out and got some chips at lunch time, and then Lucy went to see Mrs Chick and Mr Poynton. We even got out the old red biscuit tin — and they were still as crunchy as anything.

The weirdest part was leaving, and locking up again. It was dark by then, and we hadn't a torch. Lucy and I waited outside while William turned off the electricity and the house went into darkness. Depressing. Awful.

Thanks for listening.

OLIVER

Nov 21st Sunday

Dear Shrink,

Not a lot to report. Spent quite a bit of time with Mark, who seems to have missed me yesterday. I've told him that he can come with us next weekend if we go there. He said that when he's got his house with a swimming pool and Rolls Royces, I can visit him. Sounds mad, I know, but you've got to understand he's never had a real home.

I overheard Lucy telling Billy about the Shred today: "*And* she keeps a budgie prisoner in a cage!" She's bought some postcards and says she's going to send them to Chick and Poynton.

Billy's a really nice little kid. He goes into tantrums sometimes, but so does Lucy. He looks at Lucy as if he were a little faithful dog. I didn't ask him about his background as this must obviously be a painful subject, but I did ask Kate. The story about his mother dying in a fire was made up. Kate says kids often make up this kind of thing. They do it partly to attract attention, but mostly because the idea of a parent dead is actually less painful than the idea that they have rejected you. She says sometimes kids end up half-believing their own stories. She says that Billy's mother has several children, but not by the same fathers, and in Billy's case his father was a Jamaican that his mother hardly even knew, and lost track of long ago. She says two more of the children are in care in a different home. Apparently they were split up because the other two are older than Billy, and used to bully him and beat him up. That was all he needed. I've told Lucy that I'll back her up in asking him to stay when Mum and Dad get back.

When they get back. It's depressing, not even having a date to look forward to. If something went wrong, they could even be back next month. There again, if something went *really* wrong, they might not come back at all.

The minute I wrote that last sentence I wished I hadn't. You shouldn't put that sort of thing into words. Perhaps you might think this superstitious, but I think most

168

people feel the same. And going back and crossing it out won't cancel it. Damn. I don't stop to think enough, that's my trouble.

Keep your fingers crossed, Shrink.

Love,
OLIVER

Nov 23rd Tues

Dear Shrink,

Sorry about yesterday. I honestly didn't have time. If I wanted to cheat, I could always write an entry now. But that would defeat the whole object of this journal, which is meant to be total honesty. (In case you were wondering!)

At school today I realized with a shock that it's only a month till Christmas — we started practising for the Carol Concert.

But what I really am worried about is Lucy. She was babbling on to me earlier this evening about this cut-out Father Christmas they're making as a frieze, and crackers for the school party. She was going on about Christmas in general when I realized with a shock that she is taking it for granted that we'll all be back home for it, with Mum and Dad!

Now this is a fact you're going to find very interesting. I do myself. Mum went to a lot of trouble breaking Lucy in gently to the idea that they'd still be away at Christmas. (She did not, of course, know that we wouldn't even be at home.) And to give Mum her due, she bought a whole box of new Christmas tree decorations, not to be opened till December 20th, some

169

cassettes of carols, crackers and Christmas cards. (Having lived some time ago, you might wonder where she got hold of all these in September. The answer is that Woollies start Christmas at the end of the summer hols. It's working its way steadily backwards to Easter, Dad says.)

I also happen to know that there are presents for us all, wrapped ready. Lucy, William and me all know this. So how come when she's talking about Christmas, she means the usual family one?

Don't tell me. I think I know. And it's not good news. She's blocking out the knowledge that we won't have Christmas at home, because it's too painful for her to bear.

Bloody hell. I wish you could tell me what to do. Lucy's a really funny character, the whole family realizes this. What you might call "highly strung". So who's going to break it to her, and how will she react?

I really could kill Mum and Dad. They can't have thought what their going off was going to do to us. Even if Barty hadn't died, and all this happened to us, it was a rotten thing to do to be away over Christmas. This might be Lucy's last Christmas when she believes in Santa Claus. After all, for Pete's sake, kids only have a few years for hanging up stockings, and it's never the same afterwards. I know that. I enjoy Christmas all right, in fact I really love it. But a kind of mystery goes out of it once you find out.

I solemnly swear that if ever I have any children I will never, except for an Act of God, leave them at Christmas. And nobody can call an Amazon trip an Act of God.

170

And talking of God, I may as well tell you that I've started praying. I used to when I was younger, but had given it up. Anyway, I've taken it up again. It can't do any harm. I won't tell you what I'm praying for, in case it doesn't come true.

Love

OLIVER

Nov 24th Wed

Dear Shrink,

Carrying on from what I told you yesterday I had a talk with William today about Lucy and Christmas. He said that in his opinion the truth would dawn slowly on Lucy as Christmas gets nearer, and that I'm being somewhat melodramatic talking about breaking it to her. I may as well tell you that this advice leaves me cold.

I know full well that William keeps his head better in an emergency than I do. I know this. I don't deny it. But he doesn't take how people *feel* into account enough. Even his own feelings don't seem all that strong. For instance, I thought he'd be more upset about Carol, considering he was supposed to be in love. In love hell. People in love who get separated from their beloved are supposed to be in despair. Well, if he is, you could have fooled me. As a matter of fact he was talking to a girl when I found him at lunchtime, and they looked pretty thick to me. And this is no doubt why he hasn't got time to talk to me properly.

Oh, well. I won't go into all that again. But just one more item. He did say that at home he's got two envelopes Mum left with him. One is money for

Christmas, and the other, apparently, only to be opened "in case of emergency". *Now* he tells me! I ask you! So this isn't an emergency? No, he says, it is not. So what has to happen for an emergency? Me to get bubonic plague? Lucy kidnapped by a hooded gunman? Or perhaps a nuclear explosion?

Well, we'll pick up the Christmas money at the weekend. I'll have to start thinking what to get people. I say "people", but there's really only William and Lucy. I'll get Mark something, and perhaps Billy. And obviously something for the Warners.

'Night, Shrink

Love

OLIVER

25th Nov Thurs

Dear Shrink,

I'm beginning to get fed up with living in this place. *You* might forget there are eight other people besides us, because I don't mention them very often, except Mark and Billy. But it's not so easy for me to forget. It's non-stop row from morning till night. In fact, more like a continuation of school than home. Kids are always running up and down stairs (which you'll remember aren't carpeted) shrieking and yelling. There's this girl called Louise who's fifteen, and who only needs a flashing light on her head and she could set up as a foghorn. She and this other girl, Tracy, who's about the same age, are always going into fits of laughter, even at mealtimes. And I quite often get the impression it's me they're laughing at. Not to mention that they both reek of scent. Really sickly. At school, of course, it's easy enough to get away from their kind, or ignore them. But not when you live under the same roof. It must be hard enough for Kate and John as it is. I wouldn't have their job for a million a year.

You'd be interested in the inmates, all right. Not me. I've got my own problems.

Goodnight
OLIVER

Nov 26th Fri

Dear Shrink,

Today a terrible blow fell. The Warners are leaving. They're leaving a week on Sunday. John made a little speech after supper and told us the reasons. One is that apparently Kate's mother died earlier this year (most of the kids knew this, but not us) and now her father is ill and she wants to live nearby so that she can look after him. The other is that she's expecting a baby. I suppose she knows whether or not she is, but she certainly doesn't look it to me. I mentioned this to Mark later on, and he told me that with first babies it often doesn't show for ages.

John said how he and Kate always thought of us as their family as much as their own relations, and so forth. I doubt it. Would anybody leave their own children for good to go and look after their old father? Like hell they would.

Ah well, I suppose it's the way the cookie crumbles.

173

Here today, gone tomorrow. Hail and farewell. You get used to it in the end.

Later

Dear Shrink,

Talk about comings and goings! (A bit of a coincidence that this was the last subject I talked about earlier.) That Tracy I told you about is leaving, and guess who's coming here in her place? William! It'll be great. Much easier to keep us as a proper family. I don't think I realized till I heard this news how lonely I'd felt with just me and Lucy here. Don't get me wrong. She's really good company, and makes me laugh a lot, but I can't discuss any problems with her. She's too young. In any case, it wouldn't be fair, and also in any case, quite a few of my problems are to do with her.

I think William being here will help my sense of identity. You know, what I was telling you earlier, about it all being so strange that I began to wonder who I am. He will also share some of the responsibility for old Albertine.

Nobody really knows why Tracy is leaving. Mark says she's going to have a baby. Her? The mind boggles. At least there'll be less shrieking around here, as I can't see William going round with Louise and her scent bottle.

I've asked Mark if he'd like to come along with us to the house tomorrow. He seemed quite chuffed. Billy's coming as well. The only thing is that the Warners want us home by lunchtime. They're not being spoilsports. As they say, we are their responsibility. Anyway, I wasn't too keen on being there after dark.

I'll leave you to digest all this news. See you tomorrow.

Love

OLIVER

Nov 28th Sunday

Dear Shrink,

I hope you don't think I'm slipping, missing two days in one week. Some days there honestly isn't time to write to you, and yesterday was one of them. I've just had an enormous roast pork lunch and am feeling somewhat dozy, so I've propped myself up on the bed to write this.

We went to the house. If anything, it was weirder than last time, with Mark and Billy being there. In a way, to be perfectly honest, it was embarrassing. Our motive in asking them had not been to show off, but I felt as though it was. And you'd have to be a pretty rotten kind of person to be capable of showing off to people who have never even had a real home at all, let alone one like ours. If I go right to the depths of honesty, I suppose at the back of my mind I *did* hope that Mark and Billy would tell all the other kids that we did have a home, because sometimes they think we're making it up, especially the ones at Highlands. This is probably a case of judging others by yourself. They all tell some very tall stories which I won't actually call lies, but obviously are. Or perhaps fantasy would be a better word. I have fantasies myself. The difference is I don't say them out loud and pretend they're true.

There was a difference in their reactions. Billy was

175

pop-eyed and excited, and said "fab" and "brill" a lot. When he got up to Lucy's room, and saw all her stuff laid out, he just stood there and stretched his eyes till I thought they'd drop out, and said "Jesus Christ!" Lucy actually gave him several things to keep.

Mark was quite different. In a way he quite irritated me. Once he'd been there about half an hour, he kept roaming all over the house with his hands in his pockets, and saying "Ve-ery nice", pronouncing "very" as if it were two separate words. He gave the impression of somebody trying not to seem impressed. He actually asked if he could "go for a spin" in Dad's car. William asked him if he had a licence, and he said he didn't need one, he *knew* how to drive. So does William, for that matter, he practises on an old aerodrome. Dad says he could pass his test any time he wanted — except that he can't because of his age. Nor can Mark — he's not seventeen yet. When he said this, Mark just shrugged, and said he didn't see what difference a few months made. I don't suppose it does, if it comes to that. It's just illegal, that's all. Mark and William don't get on all that well. I think this is because they're nearer to each other in age, and there's a rivalry between them.

William got the two envelopes and we opened the one marked "Christmas". There were twenty pounds each in it! There was also a card from Mum and Dad. There was quite a long message in it. William read it out. It was eerie. The house was cold and dark and unlived in, and Mum and Dad were millions of miles away in hot sunshine, but it was just as if we could hear their voices speaking. Lucy started to cry, and I had a job not to. At the end Mark said "Very nice!" for about the millionth time. You can go off people.

I'll quickly tell you that after dinner today Kate and John told us they'd have a farewell party the next Saturday. They told us the name of the new people — Frost. John said "Frosty by name, but not by nature!" meant as a joke, but it left me cold. (Ho ho!) They're arriving next Saturday morning. This probably means we shan't get home.

Love
OLIVER

Nov 29th Mon

Dear Shrink,

White rabbits! I've been practising my guitar for the last hour, and it's made me feel better. You might ask why I needed to. Well, I think it's a lot of things put together. The Warners leaving, and thinking about Loose Change (my group, remember) and wondering whether they'll still want me in it when I've been away so long (though the name was my idea), and also quite a lot of aggro at school.

If our motives in taking the other two home on Sunday had been bad ones, it certainly would have bounced back on us. The word has evidently gone round. Some of the kids I'd got on OK with up to now have been ganging up and talking about me — I can tell that. It's not paranoia, I assure you. And I kept hearing the word "snob". William says it was the same for him.

Am I fed up with all this! I just wish to God Mum and

Dad would come back. I even wish one of them would get ill, so's they'd *have* to. This might sound heartless, but *they* were heartless, dumping us like this. Most of the other kids here at Highlands (and other kids at school, for that matter) are on their own because of circumstances beyond control. But our parents actually *chose* to dump us. I call it bloody selfish.

I'll finish now

OLIVER

Nov 30th Tues

Dear Shrink,

It's definitely getting worse at school, and here as well, to some extent. At school they've started imitating the way I talk, plus remarks like "Aren't we posh?" and "Lah-di-dah-di-dah!" and so forth. *We* can't help the way we talk, for heaven's sake. Nobody can. And I think this very peculiar. Now if I started imitating someone who, say, had a really strong accent so that you could hardly tell what he was saying, this would be thought really rotten. And rightly so. Of course it would be. But because we've got accents which they call "posh" (though I don't see it myself — as a matter of fact, I've never thought about it till now) it's supposed to be all right for them to gang up and make fun of us. It makes you think there really isn't any justice in the world. And same with our house. They're making remarks about that as well — and the two cars. Whereas if we made fun of someone who lived in a hovel — again, that's not on. Hell fire. What can I do?

What makes it worse is that I'm sure Mark is to blame

178

for all this. I should doubt whether Billy has said much. But I now get the feeling that Mark has it in for us since he went home with us. I think he's probably also exaggerating to make us sound richer than we are. We aren't *really* rich, for God's sake, only by comparison with some people. It's a horrible feeling that Mark has turned against me. I really thought he was my friend. And the worst thing is, that when he does see me, he pretends to be nice, and this is really sickly, and reminds me of Uriah Heep in *David Copperfield*.

It's a good job I've got you, Shrink. At least you'll never let me down. Writing to you is one of the best ideas I've ever had in my life.

Love

OLIVER

Dec 1st Wed

Dear Shrink,

The days seem to crawl by this week. And when I'm at school I wish I were at Highlands, and vice versa. That foul Cliff has obviously told about Lucy wetting the bed, and he's either made it sound as if I did as well, or else some of the others are pretending to think this. As a result, you can imagine some of the remarks I'm getting. I've been in three fights today. As a rule I hate fighting, and I've never really had to, until now. I hate the idea that I'm being forced to be someone I'm not at all. Mum and Dad have always said that you should be able to settle things without fighting. It's all very well for them to talk. I don't suppose that people kept saying "*Piss* off!" amongst other things a million times a day to them.

The only good thing is that up to now Lucy seems OK at her school, and I'm sure no one's been making that kind of remark to her, or she'd have told me. If she does run up against it, I'll sure as hell bash that Cliff Chivers' head in.

I wish you were really here, Shrink, to help me.

Love,
OLIVER

Dear Shrink,   Dec 3rd Fri

Sorry I didn't write yesterday. I'm not even really in the mood for it tonight. We've been getting things ready for the party tomorrow. The only thing is, it isn't a party, if you see what I mean. We can't be excited about it, or look forward to it, because it means goodbye to Kate and John. Some of the ones who've been here longer must feel it even more. We've all put together, and bought them a digital travelling alarm and also we've got a white cyclamen. I suppose the Frosts may be all right, but I doubt it. I used to be quite an optimist before all this lot started. Now, if anything goes right, I wonder what the catch is.

I'll write again tomorrow (or Sunday) I promise, to tell you about everything — the party and the Frosts, and so on. Mark says he's got a present of his own for Kate and John — something very special he says. Nice of him, you've got to admit. Especially as I don't suppose he'll ever see them again after tomorrow.

See you soon,

Love,
OLIVER

Dear Shrink,

This you are not going to *believe!!* God, what a day! I hardly know where to start. But I'll tell you straight off *what* has happened, and then fill in the details. MARK HAS RUN AWAY!!!! We've had the police in and reporters and everything, and the whole day has been a total shambles.

I'll now take a deep breath and try to write things more clearly. I do get excited, I admit it. As a matter of fact it's nearly 11 pm now, and I still don't feel as if I could go to sleep for hours yet.

The first time anyone noticed Mark was missing was at breakfast. Kate asked William to go and wake him — thinking he'd overslept. Then William came back and said he wasn't there. He didn't say "His bed hasn't been slept in" as it does in thrillers. This for the simple reason that at Highlands we all make our own beds.

Nobody took all that much notice at this stage. I said to Kate and John, "I'm not really giving away any secrets, but he did tell me he was giving you a leaving present of his own — something really special, he said. It's something to do with that, I bet."

Probably on an ordinary day more notice would have been taken of it, but of course we were all caught up in preparations for the party and the arrival of the Frosts, and of course Kate and John must have been in an absolute whirl.

When he didn't turn up for lunch either, Kate and John really began to worry. They didn't say so, but you could tell. They both went up to his room, leaving us all eating, and found something William had missed earlier. At least, it's not really fair to say he missed it, because he wasn't supposed to be looking for it.

It was a note from Mark. It said: "Dear Kate, thanks for everything. I shan't be back. This is my farewell present to you." And then just signed "Mark".

Absolute babel then broke out, as you can imagine. I really have got a job on now sorting it all out so that you'll get the picture. I honestly can't remember the exact order everything happened in. I think John rang the office first, and then the police. All of us were hanging about trying to find out what was going on. That Louise I told you about said, "He'll never get away. Nobody ever does. I tried it three times."

"He's older than you," I told her. "And he's got quite a bit of money, he must have. He's been saving for ages. He told me so."

I didn't tell her about the Rolls Royces and the swimming pool. Then one of the others said, "*This* is a smack in the eye for Kate. Her little blue-eyed boy hooking it today."

I wanted to know what that meant, so they told me. Apparently when Mark first arrived at Highlands Kate had really taken him under her wing. No one knew why, and no one knew exactly where he'd come from. She'd get him to help her with various things, and also spent a lot of time in the evenings talking to him, or playing table tennis or darts, and so forth. Some of the others had been quite jealous — you could tell that from the way they talked.

Louise said, "It must have been because he'd run

away from somewhere else. That's what they did with me. Tried to butter me up, so's I wouldn't do it again."

It turned out that she was right. We picked up all kinds of things during the day, things we overheard. Everyone was in such a state they weren't really bothering about what we heard and what we didn't.

I gathered that although the police were going to watch out for him, at this stage they wouldn't do much. This is because no crime has been committed, and he's over sixteen. The Frosts arrived in the middle of the afternoon, and a fine welcome it was for them. I don't say much about them at the moment, except that my heart sank. First impression. Take with a pinch of salt, I suppose. Older than the Warners. Old-fashioned-looking.

There were reporters in the afternoon. They wanted to interview us all, but only Kate and John spoke to them. I wonder where he's gone. Where will he sleep tonight? Imagine it — the dark and the cold and the loneliness.

We had the party, but it was spoilt before it began. The food was certainly good — real cream cakes, for one thing. We gave the Warners our presents, and they both made a speech and Kate was crying. Then they left.

The place seemed suddenly empty when the door closed behind them. We all went off to our separate rooms as if by an unspoken agreement. I guess we all cried. I did. Not too much. I guess I'm getting hardened.

I found out from the others that Mark wouldn't normally have been at Highlands. Usually people leave at sixteen, and get their own places. He was a special case. What happened, I think, is that the Warners, and especially Kate, made a special effort to win his

183

confidence. (Don't forget he had run away from places before.) And when they announced out of the blue that they were leaving, he felt betrayed. Personally, I don't blame him. I think it's how I would have felt. Obviously it's difficult to put myself in his shoes because until now I've had a normal family life. But he has never had a real home, and perhaps he thought he had at last found one here at Highlands. I just don't know. I expect you do.

Dear old Shrink, I wish you were here.

Love
OLIVER

Dec 5th Sunday

Dear Shrink,

It was weird to wake up today. (I woke early — it's now seven thirty, and an hour to go till breakfast.) I lay here thinking that when I went down Kate and John wouldn't be there. Then I wondered what Mum and Dad were doing, which I don't think about a lot, funnily enough. I *think* about them, all right — about the past, and what it will be like when they get back. But I don't visualize exactly what they are doing at any particular moment. For all I know, it's the middle of the night in the Amazon, and they're both fast asleep and dreaming of home.

And then I thought about Mark, and wondered how *he* felt today, and where he spent the night. I imagined him wandering about in the cold and wet, dodging into doorways whenever a police car appeared. I expect he thought running away would be an adventure. He was setting out to find fame and fortune and his swimming pool and Rolls Royces. But at two o'clock in the morning it must have all seemed very far away, wherever he was. Poor old Mark. I hope his dreams do come true.

Ah well. Nearly breakfast now. I'll go down and inspect the Frosties.

Love

OLIVER

6 pm Sunday

Shrink, you aren't going to believe what's happened now. Or perhaps you are. Perhaps you won't be surprised. Oh God. I can't write it. I feel sick. Tell you tomorrow.

Dec 6th Monday

Dear Shrink,
Sorry about last night. I think that when I tell you you'll understand.

The police came round yesterday. Our house has been broken into. And Dad's car has been stolen. Mrs Fowles heard it being driven off early yesterday morning, and went round to see what was happening.

Now I know where Mark spent the night. Two nights. William and I went with the police to the house. They wanted us to tell them what was missing. They wouldn't let Lucy go, and I can see why. The whole place was a shambles. Drawers pulled out, glasses and china smashed, paint daubed on the walls, upholstery slashed. I was literally nearly sick. He'd slept in my bed. I could kill him. He'd scrawled "Thanks a million" on the wall. In fact, I now feel that we haven't a real home any more, what with first Barty dying there, and now this. I feel as if it's tainted.

William and I were so knocked out at first that we could hardly take it in, let alone tell what was missing. But gradually we began to realize. William's hi-fi, for a start. If only Mark hadn't been able to drive, and pinched Dad's car, he'd have had to stick to things he could carry. What made me really sick (amongst other things) was that he'd been through all Mum's things as well, and left most of them lying all over the place. Her fur coat had gone, right enough, and most of her jewellery. Actually, he won't get as much as he thinks for that. Mum is very into ecology, and the fur is imitation. And she is not into diamonds and pearls and such like, either. Most of her jewellery she only chose because it was pretty, not because it's worth anything. I have seen her buy bangles and rings in Woolworth's.

Luckily there isn't a black market for Lego, so Lucy's things were safe. Good job she rescued her Money Snail, though. And to think we laughed at her when she said we might be burgled!

I forgot to mention at the beginning, Mrs Frost (she said to call her Marge, and she is certainly somewhat oily) came with us. She was tut-tutting all over the place as you can imagine. "What a shame!" she kept saying. You can say that again.

Oh Shrink, I know you have far worse cases than ours, but it all feels pretty terrible to me at the moment. I keep telling myself that in a few months I'll be able to look back on all this and laugh, but I must admit it's difficult to hang on to this. Still — stout heart, as we say to Lucy.

Steadfast tin soldier. It's all character-forming, as Dad would say. Boy, if *that's* true, we'll all have characters like nobody's business when we come out of this. Query: What has hardship done for Mark's character?

I'll leave it with you.

Love
OLIVER

PS Every cloud has a silver lining. No school today, needless to say, and none tomorrow, because William and I are being allowed to go and put the house straight.

Dec 7th Tuesday

Dear Shrink,

William and I spent the whole day back home. I'm whacked out now. Going back in there and seeing it all again was as much a shock as seeing it the first time.

Cleaning up was not a job we enjoyed. We started upstairs and worked downwards. During the day we discovered extra little touches of kindness, like the loo being stuffed with some of Mum's things, and toothpaste squirted on to the carpet. We couldn't get it off. It looks as if he took the duvet off my bed, and also the mock leopard car rug — presumably so that he can sleep in the car. I don't suppose he'd have taken the rug if he'd known where it had been. I hope old Barty rises up and haunts him. I hope she rattles in her throat right in the middle of the night.

One good job is that he didn't see where William had hidden the emergency money that day he came here with us. If he had, he'd have taken it.

This whole thing has considerably upset me. It would have been bad enough to be burgled in the ordinary way. But for it to be someone you know, someone you actually took to the house thinking he was a friend, is truly shattering.

Looking round at what he's done, you feel as if he really hates you. Stealing is one thing, but the kind of horrible acts he did are aimed at you personally. This is a horrible feeling. It makes me feel literally sick.

The funny thing is, it doesn't make me hope I'll never see him again. It makes me feel I've absolutely *got* to see him — to ask *why?* If I knew why, and if I understood how he felt, I think it might make it seem better. As it is, I'm bewildered.

Better stop now. Homework.

Love

OLIVER

Dec 8th Wednesday

Dear Shrink,

Quick impression of the Frosts, to fill you in. Thumbnail sketch. Around fifty, I should think, and very old-fashioned. Not at all like Kate and John. It even seems weird to have to call people by their Christian names (his is Harry) when they're in the grandparent category.

She, in particular, *fusses*. She talks too much. Rabbits on the whole time. And she *tells* you — Kate used to listen. The sort that thinks she knows what's best for you — best for everybody, come to that.

You should see her trying to mother Lucy and Billy. It's not that they don't *need* mothering, poor little kids, but not her brand. They hardly say anything to her except "yes" and "no", and scoot out of her way if they see her coming. She means well.

Meals are much quieter affairs now than they used to be — apart from Marge's rabbiting, I mean. This may just be because it's too soon for the ice to be broken (ouch!). I doubt it.

He's OK. She bosses him about. But he tries, you can see that. The fact that I am now stuck for anything else to say about him shows that he is not exactly Personality of the Year.

No news of Mark. But Frosty says that the police are now going to a lot more trouble to trace him than they would have done if he'd simply up and gone, and not done the burglary. I'm not sure I agree with it. I think they ought to be worried about him anyway. He's not all that old.

Frosty says they're bound to get him in the end, via the car. Personally, I could not care less about the car. In fact, if that was the only thing he'd stolen, I'd be hoping Mark got clean away with it. I'd be keeping my fingers crossed for him. After all, he did have something to run away from. Mum and Dad just walked out. People who go and leave their houses and families unattended for months on end, can hardly expect to get off scot free.

Love

OLIVER

Dec 9th Thurs

Dear Shrink,
Haven't got time for much tonight, because I went late

night shopping. The shops were absolutely packed. It was quite exciting, what with it being dark, and then all the Christmas lights and decorations, and the sound of carols floating over everywhere. Carols really get to me. Once I was in the town centre among the shops I know, and really doing exactly the same as I was doing this time last year, our whole situation seemed unreal. It seemed unbelievable that when I'd bought as much as I could carry I'd be going back here to Highlands, instead of home to show things to Mum in secret (I always get her advice, but not until *after* I've got my presents!).

I've promised to take Lucy into town on Saturday, so that she can do her Christmas shopping. I'm taking Billy too. I bet he's never had a proper Christmas in his life. I got him something tonight. I got him a model aeroplane kit, and also a woolly hat and scarf set that were selling off cheap in the market. I can just see him in them. And from what I've heard about it, the darker your skin, the more you can stand the heat, and the less cold. So I expect it'll come in handy.

Got to stop now.

Goodnight, good old Shrink,
OLIVER

Dec 10th Fri

Dear Shrink,

I may as well come right out with it. I got hauled in front of the Head today, for getting into a fight with this boy who ended up with a black eye and a bloody nose. Serve him right. I still think so, whatever anybody says. When Craddock (that's the Head's name — we call him

Fanny — amongst other things) asked why I'd gone for this boy, I wouldn't tell him. I certainly wasn't going to tell Fanny what he'd said — though no doubt you can guess. Fanny said he was "disappointed in me". I think he lives in a world of his own, there in that room lined with timetables as if it was a fighter squadron leader's control room. Luckily, he didn't seem all that interested in me. Just a name on a list, I expect. So I got off with a caution.

But I feel bad. I feel as if I'm being forced to be someone I'm not. On the other hand, this can't be true. I didn't *have* to black Paul Benson's eye. I could just have walked away. It was my own fault that I let him get under my skin.

End of the week now, anyhow. Only another five school days to go. Perhaps we might be able to get home most days in the holidays. Home. It makes you laugh.

Goodnight, Shrink.

OLIVER

11th Dec Sat

Dear Shrink,

I now think it is just as well that I only write to you, that you aren't actually here. Because you might not approve of what I'm going to tell you. I won't tell you straight away, I'll explain what led up to it.

We went shopping — William, Lucy, Billy and I. It was quite a game, really, because we had to keep swapping partners. For instance, first I went with Lucy, so that she could buy presents for Billy and William, and then Lucy went with William and Billy to buy things for me. We kept meeting every half hour by the musical clock. It was good fun. I may as well tell you what old Lucy picked. She got Billy this truly boz-eyed floppy leopard to put his pyjamas in. She said he'd like it, because it was a good excuse to have something to cuddle. "He hasn't got a Hamish," she said. By this she meant that he hadn't got a bedtime toy like this knitted object she's got that goes by the name of Hamish. (I think it might be a hobbit, or it might be a white teddy bear that went wrong — knitting isn't Mum's strong point.) Anyhow, I could follow her reasoning. If she'd bought him a furry leopard that *didn't* hold pyjamas, that would have looked babyish. But I wouldn't be surprised if he did need something to cuddle — he seems younger than Lucy is in lots of ways. Old Lucy does have quite a grip on psychology, I think you'll agree. Then for William she's got a photo frame (for a photo of his "true love" she said!) and some blank cassettes. I don't know how enchanted he'll be when she tells him what she told me. She said he can use them to record Christmas. "Because they'll *miss* this Christmas, and it'll have gone for ever, if we don't," she said. Well — yes. And certainly every Christmas since I can remember Mum and Dad have made a cassette of it — us all singing carols, and opening our presents on Christmas morning, and so forth. But it struck me, and it'll strike William, that if they had cared that much about missing a Christmas, they wouldn't have gone off in the first place. Apart from which I shouldn't think Christmas at Highlands will be a laugh a minute. (But more of this, later.)

I took Billy to find something for Lucy. He only had

192

sixty pence. I didn't want to offer to give him some in case it made him embarrassed. Luckily, this didn't arise. He picked a game that cost two pounds fifty five, and stood waving it, beaming from ear to ear. So I took his money from him and paid for it. It's pretty awful when schools can't teach people the money system. They could be robbed left and right.

Anyway, when we got back home we were in a really good mood, all laughing and clutching fish and chips as well as our parcels. Even seeing again some of the damage done by Mark didn't have much effect. Lucy got William to put some carols on a radio cassette that had been overlooked by Mark, and all of a sudden I had a great rushing feeling of Christmas — of the real Christmases we'd always had, and I think the others must have felt the same, because when I said, "Let's run away, and have a *real* Christmas!" they knew straight away exactly what I meant.

And when I say we were "seized" by the idea, I'm not exaggerating at all. I can only speak for myself, but the minute I'd said this (and I said it without even having *thought* it — it just came out) I felt the most tremendous excitement and relief I've ever had in my life. It was as if all our problems were thrown away in the twinkling of an eye. Because most of our problems are to do with other people. If we could just be left alone to be ourselves — which is what we had wanted right from the very start — then *we'd be all right*.

Lucy and I started whooping and running round the room, and Billy followed suit, though I don't expect he knew why.

We don't know how we're going to do it, but we *are*. And Billy — he's coming with us. He hardly understands what we're talking about, but he likes us, I know he does. He probably even *loves* us. And I think we love him.

We're going to have to map the whole thing out carefully. We've got time. It's obvious we can't just scarper off home and have Christmas there — it's the first place they'll look. On the other hand, they don't know about the Shack. And by the time they did find out, it would be too late. We'd have *had* our Christmas.

I expect all this has given you something to think about. It certainly has me!

Love

OLIVER

12th Dec, Sun

Dear Shrink,

Roast potato day here again! Query: Why do people on the whole only have roast potatoes on Sunday? They could have them any day of the week they liked. Must be a sort of brain-washing. *You'll* know.

I can't tell you how happy I feel. I've been making jokes all day. If you tried to analyse *why*, I think it's probably the actual prospect of having our own Christmas, but perhaps even more the feeling of being *myself* again — Oliver Edward Saxon. I've mentioned to you before the feeling of being forced to be someone I'm not, and I think also that over the weeks since Barty died, I've only been passive, a pawn in the game, helpless, at the mercy of others. Heaven help the poor kids who get years of this.

We had a council of war in William's room today. We'd both been thinking about the Shack since yesterday, and come to the conclusion it wasn't too good an idea. For one thing, it would be cold and damp, and also we'd have a job getting all the decoration, presents, grub etc down there. But William has had a brilliant idea. He says that when we leave Highlands we should go straight to the Shack. He reckons it would take the police a few days to track us down there, if we're lucky. His idea is that we'd stay there, leaving plenty of evidence that we'd been there, and then *come back home*! It's so simple, when you think of it. The police will go straight to the house when we're reported missing, find us not there, and cross it off their list! They'll spread the net wider.

Everything falls into place. For instance, the Fowleses next door always go and stay with their married daughter at Christmas, so there's no danger of them coming round.

Also, there's a secret hiding-place in the house — disguised, just as Anne Frank's was. It's in Mum's and Dad's bathroom. There's a little door at floor level, just high enough to crawl through, and on the other side is a kind of platform on the rafters. We keep suitcases in there, and Christmas decorations and all kinds of other junk. There's even a *light* in there!

Anyway, that's the broad outline of our plan. We'll fill in the other details as we go along.

I think it's going to be great being a fugitive. It's a good word, "fugitive".

Hey ho, Shrink — just think, you'll be coming with us!
Love
OLIVER

Dec 13th Mon

Dear Shrink,
Last week of school. What people say just goes off me like water off a duck's back now. I understand now why prisoners of war spent so much time digging tunnels, etc, to try to escape, even if the odds were stacked against them. Just *doing* something, planning something, makes life completely different.

William and I had quite a long discussion tonight about whether to use Mum's car. I know William's under age, and it'd be illegal, but on the other hand he can drive very well. And we wouldn't necessarily be tracked down by the registration number — let's face it, Mark's still on the loose. Nor, I might add, is anybody falling over backwards to trace him. After that first day there's been nothing in the papers or on telly. I wonder where he *is*? I hope he's OK. Now that I'm about to become a fugitive myself, I can truly sympathise with him.

Anyway, I suppose you'll be relieved to hear that we won't take the car. William looks too young. We'd have to stop to get petrol, and it would attract too much attention.

So we've decided to go by train. William's going to the station to get a timetable after school tomorrow. So the

196

plot is definitely thickening!

I even find I get on all right with the Frosts, now I know we're leaving.

Love
OLIVER

PS Gordon Bennett — wouldn't it be awful if anyone found this book? I'm going to put it under my mattress.

Dec 14th Tuesday

Dear Shrink,

More details of the Great Escape. The timing's very important. You see, we don't expect to get clear away indefinitely — there wouldn't be much chance of that. Just long enough to be away over Christmas.

What we'll do is go home on Saturday, and do shopping for food, which we'll then hide. We'll travel to Shrewsbury by the 3.22 train on Sunday. We shan't be missed until at least 6.30 (plus we shan't miss the roast — I have measured out my life with roast potatoes!). We'll get return tickets, because William says that people will be on the look-out for us when we return, whereas on the way there no one will even know we've gone. He's got a cool head, old William has, I'll give him that. We're going to split into pairs — William and Billy, and Lucy and me. So when our descriptions are issued, as I expect they will be, no one will remember seeing four of us. Good thinking.

There are several reasons why we picked Sunday. (1) because the Fowleses next door will have left by then, and they're the most likely to tell the police about the

Shack — though I'm sure they don't know exactly where it is. (2) because lots of people will be travelling the last Sunday before Christmas, and we're less likely to be noticed. (3) because we reckon the police will have tracked us down within a week or so. So we'll just spend a few nights there, and travel back home on Christmas Eve. (Another day when people will be too busy to notice us.) Five nights at the Shack will be plenty. It'll be cold and damp. There'll be food there, though, even if it is all in tins. We shan't starve, you'll be glad to hear.

Mr and Mrs Frost are always referring to one another in conversation. Marge will say, "My hubby doesn't like you to play table tennis after nine," and he will say "My wife would rather you didn't open the windows in this weather." In a weird way, you feel she's speaking for him, and he for her, like a pair of ventriloquist's dummies. Perhaps that's what marriage does to you in the end (amongst other things!). Or perhaps neither of them really wants the responsibility for us, so they each try to make out the other one's giving the order. That's more like it, don't you think, Shrink? You're the expert.

Love

OLIVER

Dec 15th Wed

Dear Shrink,

Another day nearer. Getting near countdown. It's a good job we didn't decide to go off just on the spur of the moment. We'd have hit quite a few snags. Doing it this way, we can plan the most important things. We shall

198

have to do most of our shopping for food on Saturday. Also, we'll have to pack all we need in one suitcase (including clothes for Billy) and hide it in a wardrobe.

I suppose we can only trust to luck that Billy won't let something out and give the game away. I don't think he will. He can be very solemn when you tell him things. He's got very big wide shiny eyes. I bet he'll really enjoy our Christmas. From William's and my point of view, it's really useful that Billy's coming. It will distract Lucy's attention from any aspects of things that might be a bit scary. For one thing, it'll be pitch dark when we get to the Shack. And that can be spooky even when we're with Mum and Dad, and have got the car. I tell you, Shrink, when I picture the four of us trekking down that track and over the fields, even I feel shivery. Still, there are four of us. We'll have to sing carols as we go, to keep our spirits up. And you'll be with us, of course, whether you like it or not. Gordon Bennett, what if I forgot you and *they* found you.

Cheers, Shrink!
OLIVER

Dec 16th Thurs

Dear Shrink,

We had a real surprise today — a letter from Mum and Dad! No, don't get excited — it doesn't mean they're back in civilization. It's one they wrote for us to receive at Christmas, and left with someone to post. Needless to say, it was not addressed here, but to home. But Mrs F next door had gone in to check everything was all right before they set off to her daughter's. There were some cards as well — obviously from people who didn't know they were away.

It was weird to read the letter, because we are now light years away from where we were when they left us. The weirdest part was that there was a PS telling us where Mum had left a present for Barty, and also a separate letter for Barty. It was in a sealed envelope, and we couldn't at first decide whether to open it or not. You obviously don't open other people's letters when they're alive, but I don't know about when they're dead. The subject has never come up before.

In the end William and I decided we would (we left Lucy out of it). First, because if we didn't, the logical thing then would be to send it to Barb or Janet, which didn't exactly seem like the idea of the century. And secondly because we thought there might be some instructions in it that we ought to know.

It's funny. It was nice to get our own letter, and to know that Mum and Dad were with us at least in spirit, but it was Barty's letter that made me want to cry. There *were* instructions — all kinds of funny little details — mainly about Lucy, and her letter to Father Christmas, and where to find the things that were to go into her stocking, and so on. All the little details of our Christmas — I suppose every family has their own. I mean, for instance, we always ice the cake while the King's College Carols are on in the afternoon on Christmas Eve. Lucy sticks reindeers and fir trees and Santa Clauses all over it, and all the while Mum's making the stuffing, and the smell is delicious. And then we have Christmas Eve tea by candlelight. Mum's very keen on candles, and lights them at the least excuse.

Reading that letter, I think it really must have cost them something to miss out on Lucy's last real believing Christmas. They'd really gone to some trouble. So I take back some of the things I said about them earlier. William and I have already got some little things to put in Billy's and Lucy's stockings, and now we'll be able to divide the other things between them, as well. I'm beginning to *feel* like Father Christmas!

I've just thought. Those two both have the same name. It's honestly only just struck me. Query: Why is it impossible to think of William as Billy, and Billy as William!

I'll leave it with you!

Love
OLIVER

Dec 17th Friday

Dear Shrink,

End of school. I actually got some cards, which amazed me. And Lucy and Billy had a party at their school, and both got presents from Father Christmas — a doll for Lucy, and a painting-by-numbers set for Billy. Frankly, I think they might as well swap. You don't catch old Albertine playing with dolls. I sure as hell bet she ends up doing half that painting.

This evening we put up the decorations at Highlands. Frankly, I felt somewhat of a fraud, pretending to be excited about it. I spent quite a lot of the time blowing up balloons, which helped to relieve my feelings. I really do

201

have about a million butterflies flapping around in my stomach.

While we were doing the decorations, I thought about Mark, and wondered where he was. What kind of Christmas will he have, I wonder? None at all. You can't have Christmas unless you're with people you know and love, and who know and love you. Poor old Mark. I wonder whether *you* think there's such a thing as fairness in life, Shrink? It's really depressing to think there might not be.

I won't think about it any more. I am considerably excited, positively elevated. Whatever happens, whether things go right or not, we aren't committing a crime, and it will be an adventure of our own making. A change from being O. Saxon — Pawn.

Love
OLIVER

Sat Dec 18th

Dear Shrink,
The problem is (though obvious, if you think about it) that the more there is to tell, the less time there is to tell it in. But as we are now on the eve of the Great Escape all the historic detail must be painstakingly recorded! In any case, I should think I'll find it hard to get to sleep tonight. Think — this time tomorrow we shall be on the run!

William and I were running feverishly round all day doing the shopping. We had lists as long as the M1. We left Billy and Lucy at the house, making Christmas cards — they'd never have stood the pace. I hope we haven't forgotten anything — I never *realized* how much there was to get. Memo: next time Mum gets into a lather just before Christmas, remember this!

We put a lot of the stuff in tins and packets in the larder as usual — nothing to arouse suspicion. But the fresh stuff (including the turkey) we've hidden in the roof, behind that door I told you about. The turkey is frozen, and weighs about sixteen pounds, so we reckon it'll be just nicely thawed out by the time we need it. We put it in a roasting tin. As William pointed out, if it started leaking as it thawed, and dripped down through the ceiling below, the police would think they had a murder on their hands.

I must say that William does have a good head in a crisis. I would not particularly want to say this to his face, because his opinion of himself is already considerable. But, for instance, he dug out an old fur-lined anorak of mine for Billy to wear. The point is, Billy always wears this kind of hooded duffle in red tartan, and as William pointed out, descriptions are bound to be circulated. That tartan job would have stood out a mile.

There were quite a few more cards at the house — including one from Carol. William waxed quite confidential about this. It turns out that they have spoken a few times on the 'phone. Reading between the lines, I reckon William has an ulterior motive in this Escape, besides the one of having our own Christmas. I think he thinks that when there is a big drama about our disappearing, and things in the papers and on TV she'll see him in a romantic light. He could well be right about

203

this. She'll probably come on telly sobbing and begging him to give himself up. She'll probably even think he's done it because of her. This is the way many girls' minds work. Not all girls, naturally. I reckon old Albertine will be all right. There again, she does have a strong sense of the dramatic, and for all I know, would make a bigger scene on television than anybody.

While on the subject of Lucy, she's done something really typical. She suddenly came over all sad and sobbing about how poor Mr and Mrs Frost will feel when they find us gone. She does have a point. They are a harmless enough pair, without being personalities of the century, and Lucy being how she is had built up quite a relationship with Marge, and had made her a pincushion at school. All the kids made one, apparently, to give their mothers at Christmas. Anyway, she wrapped this bright blue object up, with the holly paper all sogged up from tears dripping on it. Then she made a Christmas card and wrote inside: "Happy Christmas to Mr and Mrs Frost. PS We did not (underlined about a million times) run away because we don't like you, because we do. Please don't be upset, we have only gone on an adventure." Then about two million kisses. She wanted to leave it on her bedside table just before we leave tomorrow, but William said they might find it too soon. So in the end she agreed to leave it under her pillow.

I've just broken off to check my list again. Here it is: clothes (obviously!), torch and spare battery, matches, chocolate, portable rado/casette, plus tapes of carols.

Hadn't finished the list. Nearly went into fits — in came Marge, saying wasn't it about time I put my light out? Said I was writing my diary, which is, of course, true.

'Night.

OLIVER

Sun Dec 19th

Dear Shrink,

Oh Shrink, we're on the train! Now, this minute, as I write this! Lucy's sitting opposite counting churches and horses. It's amazing, the feeling I have. It's as if for weeks and weeks I'd been numb, or dead, and had suddenly come to life again. (Perhaps not suddenly, because I think this feeling started the minute we hit on our plan.) But to be actually sitting here, free, here because I want to be, and not because somebody said so, is incredible. I'm sure William feels the same. We bought our tickets and came through the barrier at the station in pairs, as we'd decided, but once on the platform I could see him and Billy further down, and our eyes met, and I *knew* we were both feeling the same thing.

Everything went like clockwork. When I first woke and looked out I nearly had a fit when I saw everything white. What if there had been a blizzard, and the trains weren't running? But it was only a thin sprinkling, and I listened to the weather on my radio, and although snow was forecast, they didn't sound very worried.

During the morning William smuggled the case and duffles out, and left them behind the wall near the gate. We had a smashing dinner — beef and Yorkshire pudding, followed by mince pies. I had a job to force any of it down on account of those butterflies under my belt, but the funny thing was, Lucy and Billy, who I'd have thought would have given the game away if anyone did, were acting as if they hadn't a care in the world. Except that they weren't acting, it was genuine. I suppose this is because when you're young — a real kid, I mean — everything in your life is arranged for you, and you do it regardless, without question. You really are a pawn in the game. you accept everything that comes along, because you have no choice. Even now, old Albertine is doing exactly what she always does when she's on a train. And I don't suppose she's even given a thought to the dangers that may lie ahead. Well, I'm glad.

Every now and then the butterflies flap as I picture the scene at Highlands at this very minute, and wonder whether we've been missed yet. The sky is becoming a dense, pale grey. I think it may snow.

Later

Oh Shrink, I can't tell. Not now. I'm still dazed and my bones ache.

Later

Dear Shrink,

I'll try to tell things the way they happened. We're here at the Shack, but not in the way we imagined. And we're not alone.

It was already snowing when we left the train. We needn't have worried about disguises. I don't think anybody gave us a second glance. They were all hellbent for their own Christmases.

After a quick confab we decided to risk taking the bus out of Shrewsbury. We had intended to walk (it's around four miles) but that was before the snow. William and Billy sat together and got off the stop before the one for the Shack, and Lucy and I got off the stop after. Both William and I had keys, so that whoever got there first could open up.

Lucy and I stood and watched the lights of the bus disappear, and the dark and the silence were enormous. This is an aspect of life at the Shack that comes as a shock every time we go there. Once you have left the road three fields and several copses away, you might as well be living in the Stone Age. We could only use one torch. Both my hands were needed for the luggage. I told Lucy to walk ahead of me shining it, and I'd follow. I could see she wasn't too keen on this. Once my eyes became readjusted I realized that it was not absolutely dark. A faint light seemed to come off the snow, like a halo.

"Let's try and race the others," I said. The faster she went, the less she was likely to imagine things. I wasn't frightened at all. Who was likely to be lurking in the snow-covered fields at that time?

We began to sing carols — not very well, because we were somewhat breathless. I suppose the journey took around a quarter of an hour, though time seemed to disappear in the darkness, it was the beam of light from the torch that was important. It began to snow again, heavily.

"Right, Albertine!" I said. "This is our cue. *Good King Wenceslas* — as loud as you can!"

We stomped along through the whirling flakes,

yelling the words:

> *In his master's steps he trod,*
> *Where the snow lay dinted . . .*

As we finished, I realized we were nearly there, and above my own breathing I could hear another sound.

"Stop!" I said. "Listen!"

We stopped and could hear, very faintly — *Good King Wenceslas.* Weird, like a long-drawn-out echo of ourselves. And a sort of coincidence, I suppose.

"Quick!" I said. "It's them. We've made it first."

We didn't see the Shack until we were almost upon it, we were blinded by the dizzy swirl of snow. I dumped the bags and fished the key from my anorak pocket. The minute I put it in the lock I knew something was wrong. It wouldn't turn either way. I pushed the handle. The door was already open.

Now I've got to admit to being a coward. Without even thinking I grabbed hold of Lucy and began to pull her with me in the direction of the singing voices — *Hark the Herald Angels* it was now.

"What? What're you doing? Let *go!*"

Lucy dropped the torch and I snatched it up and kept going. Hot and cold tides were washing up and down my spine. I took a quick look back over my shoulder, but saw only the wall of snow. We ran practically headlong into the others. I yelped.

"Hey — what the? — where d'you think you're going, idiot?"

"William! The Shack!" The words would hardly come. My tongue was tied by cold and shock. He stared at me.

208

"The door — it was already open!"

I was shuddering. We all stood ther goggle-eyed and helpless.

"Someone's broken in, then," William said at last. "Not much to take, anyway. Come on."

"But — but what if someone's *in* there!"

"Was there a light?"

"No. At least, I don't think so. But — "

"Come *on*, then!" He sounded mad, but I guessed he was as frightened as I was. We all turned and trudged back towards the Shack, following the prints Lucy and I had made, though they were already filling in fast.

There were four of us this time, and two torches. We stopped dead only a few yards from the Shack.

"Help! Help!"

A terrible cold crawling went down my spine.

"Help! Help!"

A faint voice from the other side of that door. I noticed something I hadn't seen before. A ladder was placed up against the roof. Whatever for? The door was forced. My mind wouldn't work.

"Come on!" William's teeth were chattering, too. Lucy and Billy stood huddled together, staring-eyed and silent.

William pushed open the door. I was right behind him. The torch beam went ahead of us and picked out something white and shining, something dangling —

I let out a terrified yelp and turned to run, but William grabbed me tightly by the arm.

"Who's there?" I hardly recognized his voice.

I was looking at the dangling skeleton with its socket-

209

eyed skull.

"Here!" A faint voice came. Slowly William swung the beam and it picked out a huddled heap of blankets on the floor. And a face. Mark's.

Oh Shrink, I can't even find the words to tell you my feelings. I was amazed, staggered — the last person in the world I'd ever have expected to see there! And mixed in with that, fury that he should gatecrash our Christmas, and then an uneasiness, a feeling that something was seriously wrong.

He gave a slight smile. A shadow smile. Then he made a movement as if to get up, gave a terrible cry, and keeled over sideways. We stood there like statues, staring at the crumpled heap in the arc of the torch. William moved first. He bent over Mark.

"Looks as if he's fainted. He's obviously hurt."

"Can't we put a light on?" Lucy asked. "I don't like it in the dark. And I'm cold."

William said, "Hell's *bells* — what's he *doing* here? And what's the idea of that skeleton dangling up there? I hadn't even realized he'd pinched it. Get it down, Oliver."

"What about him?" I said, meaning Mark.

William shrugged.

"Not a lot we can do. Not till he comes round. If we move him, we might do more harm than good."

I knew that was true. I'd read it somewhere. I remembered vaguely other things.

"Shouldn't we cover him with blankets and get some hot sweet tea?"

"It's *us* that could do with some hot sweet tea."

William was grim. It reminded me of another scene. Barty on the stairs. Even the same mock-leopard-skin rug was there. I could see blood on his coat. He can't die, I thought. Not another body under that same rug. That's taking coincidence too far.

Then there was a light. The relief was enormous. The beam of a torch is such a narrow one, and it's always dark behind you. You can feel the dark over your shoulder.

"That's better," William said. "Now the fire."

Soon that was hissing, too. It seemed almost cosy in there, except for the silent figure on the floor. But for that, we'd be feeling triumphant now, and safe. Mission accomplished.

"There doesn't seem to be a spare cylinder," William said. "I expect he's used the other. We'll have to go easy on the gas."

We cut down the skeleton and fetched things from outside. They were already coated with snow. Over the white fields I could hear a fox barking. Billy and Lucy were crouching by the fire with their fingers spread. It was eerily quiet, except for the hissing of the gas. I delved into my haversack for the radio.

"Get the weather forecast," I said. What I really meant was "Let's fill the silence."

I switched on. Nothing. I twiddled the dial impatiently.

"What the hell?" I said. "I put new batteries in."

The minute I'd said it, I knew. I'd bought new batteries, I'd taken the old ones out . . .but . . . I pressed the release catch. Empty. No batteries at all, not even worn-out ones. The one time in my life when I'd really needed that radio, except as a background, and it was dumb.

"Hell! Hell!" I could have cried. I really could.

"What?" William came over and looked. "You fool!" he said. "You *fool!*"

There was nothing I could say.

"Properly cut off now. Don't even know whether we've been missed, whether they're looking, whether we're going to be snowed in here for days on end, whether — "

"I'm hungry." It was Lucy. "And you are as well, aren't you, Billy?"

"I'll get them something," I said. I wanted to make it up to William, even if that was impossible. Anyhow, finding and opening tins and heating food was a normal, everyday thing to do. A comfort. We all had beans on toast. We'd brought bread with us.

By the time we'd finished and were drinking our tea, Mark still hadn't come round. We watched the steam rising from the sleeping bags in front of the fire. We were all going to have to sleep in that one room. We couldn't afford the gas to light and heat another. Billy seemed happy enough, but I noticed that Lucy kept glancing at Mark. I did myself. How badly hurt was he? Was he going to come round at all? It was still quite early in the evening. He wasn't in a natural sleep.

"What d'you think happened to him?" I asked William.

"Search me. Serve him right, whatever it was. And where's Dad's car? Did you and Lucy see it?"

"Of course not. If we had, we'd have *known* it was him

in here."

"But it was snowing really thickly," Lucy said. "It could've been there and us *not* seen it."

"Ought we to get a doctor?" I said. Silly question. No telephone.

"How? Pick up the 'phone? Or trot over to Shrewsbury in this lot, I suppose, and fetch one?"

He was right.

"All I know is, he's a bloody nuisance." William never shows very much emotion, but if ever he does, it's usually fury. "Look at all the trouble we've gone to. Everything was going like clockwork. And *he* has to put his spoke in. As if he hadn't done enough harm already."

Again I said nothing. I couldn't defend Mark. On the other hand, I couldn't bring myself to condemn him. Not while he lay like that, so white and still.

"I'm listening . . ."

I froze at the sound of that faint voice.

"I can hear what you're saying."

"Are you all right?" I went and bent over him. "Mark, what happened?"

"Fell. Off the ladder. Leak in the roof."

He gave a little feeble laugh.

"What happened, though?" His face suddenly changed. It twisted with pain, he was hardly recognizable.

"Oh . . . my leg . . ."

"What about your arm? There's blood on your sleeve."

"My arm . . . my arm . . ." His head jerked from side to side. "My head. Black and dizzy . . ." Another groan.

213

A sickening groan. "Hell, my *leg* . . ."

His eyes closed again. They hadn't been properly open.

"Mark! Mark!"

There was no reply. Then, in the silence, came Lucy's voice.

"Oh Oliver, he's not going to die, is he? Don't let him die!"

"Shut up, Lucy," William said. "No one's going to die."

"Barty did! Barty did!"

"Shut *up*, will you!"

For what seemed a very long time the fire hissed. Then Mark started to speak again, except that he wasn't exactly speaking. He was muttering. I leaned nearer to catch the words.

"Not far now . . . not far . . . this is it, this must be it . . . safe now. Yes, safe now . . ."

His eyes suddenly opened again. It was a shock. But he wasn't looking at me at all. He wasn't looking at anything.

"Christmas . . . safe till after Christmas . . ."

There was silence again.

"I don't like it," Lucy said in a small voice. "And Billy doesn't either. Thought you said we were going to have a real Christmas. Poor Billy. We shouldn't have brought him."

"I like it." It was the first time Billy had spoken since we arrived, as far as I knew. "Honest, Lucy. I like it."

"You don't!" Lucy was nearly crying. "You're just trying not to hurt our feelings. It wasn't meant to be like

214

this, Billy, it wasn't at all. It was meant to be fun!"

"I like it," he said again. "Don't you cry, Lucy. It'll be tomorrow soon."

It really got me, the way he said that. You could just imagine how often grown-ups had said that to *him* to try to calm him down. "It'll soon be tomorrow." As if tomorrow was something magical. As if you'd wake up in the morning, and suddenly everything would be all right.

Mark began moaning. William looked over towards him but didn't move. Gingerly, I put my hand on Mark's forehead. It was burning hot. I snatched my hand away.

"Hot?"

I nodded.

"We don't even know how long he's been lying here," I said. "It could have been for days."

"It doesn't make any difference," William said. "Days or hours. There's absolutely nothing we can do about it."

"No."

I went and turned the sleeping-bags over and the steam rose again.

"They can't use these yet," I said, meaning Billy and Lucy. "Better get a game out."

"Snakes and Ladders," Lucy said quickly. She knew Billy hadn't got the hang of Monopoly yet. Besides, it might take too long. I got the game out of the cupboard, and they squatted on the floor beyond the sleeping-bags to play. William was fiddling with one of the lamps. I began writing this. There doesn't seem anything much else to do. I don't know what we'd have done if Mark *hadn't* been there, I only know it would have been

215

different. There doesn't even seem any point in unpacking. Nobody actually said so, but it looks as if Christmas is over before it has even begun. I can't feel any of the triumph and excitement I felt earlier. I feel cold and sad and I feel frightened. Mark is badly hurt. He's begun tossing his head from side to side, and muttering. I've never heard anyone being delirious, but I'm sure that's what he is. William's writing as well, now. And every now and again I see him glance over towards Mark. He doesn't say anything.

Billy has just won his third game of Snakes and Ladders.

"Come on, you two," William says. "Into those sleeping-bags. It's gone ten."

What I'm writing now is first-hand reporting, you realize. History as it happens. Billy and Lucy are bagged up now, exchanging goggle-eyed looks out of the corners of their eyes, and giggling. They don't look to me as if they're anywhere near going to sleep. William has just gone over and felt Mark's forehead. I pretended not to see him. Now he's gone to the other end of the room, in the shadows, and opened the door. A great snowy gust blows in.

"Just going outside a minute."

He's back already. He's standing looking down at Mark.

Later

Oh Shrink, William's gone. There are just the three of us now, and that moaning figure on the floor. But if *we're*

216

frightened, how must it be for William, out there in the snow and the darkness? I must put it down on paper that I think he is truly brave. Already the snow round the Shack is nearly two feet deep. And now there's a wailing, patchy wind — fitful, I expect that word is, that could be whipping up drifts as high as houses. I know they often get snowed up round here. The locals have told us so.

The very fact that William has gone out into the blizzard shows that he knows that Mark is seriously ill — dangerously, even. Oh Shrink, I'm frightened. What if he does actually die? Or wakes up screaming? Billy and Lucy whisper to each other from time to time. Whenever I look at them I see their wide-open eyes. I could go and read to them, I suppose. But somehow it doesn't seem right to be reading Spike Milligan or Lear or someone against that background muttering of pain.

Shrink, the world really can be a very dangerous place to be. Think — there we all were a few hours ago, laughing and happy and thinking that at last we were in control of our lives again after all those months, and now look. Life's in control of us, whether we like it or not.

At times, I wonder if we ever —

Later

Oh Shrink, I can't even remember what I was going to put when I broke off. There was this sudden heavy thud against the door and it flew open and Lucy screamed and it was William, soaked and gasping. He stumbled forward and fell. I rushed over to him.

"What's up? What is it?"

217

He was still gasping for breath, but he told me, in fits and starts. He didn't know how far he'd got towards the road, because out there it's all mountains and pits, he said, like a lunar landscape. Anyway, he said he'd almost decided he'd have to turn back anyway, when he'd gone over sideways and wrenched his left ankle. Lord knows how he managed to get back. If he'd actually broken his ankle, instead of spraining it, I suppose he could still be lying out there, slowly being covered in snow. It's a nightmare. All five of us are well and truly trapped now. William can't even get his wellington off. You can tell he's in agony. I'm going to look for some scissors, and cut it off. I expect his leg and foot will be swelling. I suppose I'm left in charge now, with William hurt. It's just you and me, Shrink.

Christmas Eve

Dear Shrink,

Dear, dear Shrink, I am writing this in my room back home. I can hear carols playing and Mum and Dad laughing and Lucy squealing and God's in his heaven, all's right with the world!

I couldn't write before, I really couldn't. But I wasn't going to start Christmas without letting you know that we are all safe, and happier than we've ever been in our lives, I guess. You've got to know what it's like to be unhappy to know what real happiness is, and I don't suppose any of us really had, till now.

That night, in the Shack, we really hit bottom, all of us — except Mark, who was unconscious. There seemed no way out. And you're never going to believe how we were rescued. It was enough like a miracle to *us*, so it will be even more amazing to you, who have never even heard of helicopters. The story's very complicated. But what happened is that Mum and Dad actually decided they couldn't face Christmas without us (and after all I've said about them!) and had flown home to surprise us. Think, at the very time we were on the train to Shrewsbury, they were in the air on their way home! What's known as irony, I think.

You can imagine how they felt when they found the house in darkness, and empty. Not to mention the decorations on the walls and the breakages from Mark's visit. Apparently Mum had actual hysterics, and Dad had to slap her face. He got straight on to the police, and they told him that we had been at Highlands, but had just been reported missing. This sent Mum right off again, as you can imagine. There's no doubt that they got their share of nightmare that night, too. (Query: can you have a daymare?)

Well, of course it didn't take Mum and Dad long to put two and two together, especially when they found the keys to the Shack missing. By this time, all the roads out of Shrewsbury were impassable, apparently, and the snow was still coming.

So now we come to the helicopter, which is a sort of small aeroplane but worked by propellers, and it moves rather like a dragonfly, and can land in places that can't be reached any other way.

Shrink, it was unbelievable that night, when we'd all gone very quiet out of pure fear, and then all of a sudden, right out of nowhere, there came this buzzing, louder and louder and closer and closer until it was almost deafening. And when the noise stopped, and we were all practically rigid with shock, the door burst open, and it was *Dad!*

It was *incredible!* Lucy gave one great shriek and jumped out of her bag and ran to him shouting, "Dad, Dad, Dad!" over and over again, and I burst into tears, and when I could see again through the blur I saw that William was crying, too. And I'll tell you something else. Dad was as well. We were all laughing and crying at the same time, and then there were other people there as well, and it was all so confused I can hardly remember it. I suppose that's what you call irony, as well. The greatest moment of my life, and I can't describe it!

I can't write much longer. It's Christmas Eve, remember, and our candlelight tea to come, and then the carols, and Lucy's and Billy's letters to Father Christmas. That's something I forgot to mention. Billy's here with us, and I think he's going to stay for good, and be part of the family. So one really good thing has come out of all this. We've been to see Mark in hospital, and he's going to be all right. He cried when he saw us. He's really sorry for what he did and of course there's no question of Dad making any charges against him. Poor old Mark. But I think he'll get a good Christmas in hospital.

And now our real Christmas has started, and it *is* to be a real one, beyond our wildest dreams, and the thought of it brings tears to my eyes even now. And I want to thank you, dear old Shrink, for being my friend. And I'd give anything to be able to look you in the eyes and say it, and for you to be actually here with us to share the carols and the turkey and the laughing. But you can't, and that's why I came up here to have a few quiet minutes alone with you, and thank you again from the bottom of my heart. I'll never have a better friend than you. Goodbye, dear Shrink — and a Happy Christmas!

Love
OLIVER